I0589117

Creative Texts Publishers products are available at special discounts for bulk purchase for sale promotions, premiums, fund-raising, and educational needs. For details, write Creative Texts Publishers, PO Box 50, Barto, PA 19504, or visit www.creativetexts.com

SURVIVAL SHORT STORIES 2
by Jerry D. Young
Published by Creative Texts Publishers
PO Box 50
Barto, PA 19504
www.creativetexts.com

Cover photo modified and used by license.
Credit: Darron Birgenheir

The following is a work of fiction. Any resemblance to actual names, persons, businesses, and incidents is strictly coincidental. Locations are used only in the general sense and do not represent the real place in actuality.

ISBN: 978-0-692-61454-9

FAMILY EMERGENY EXCURSION

By
JERRY D. YOUNG

FAMILY EMERGENCY EXCURSION

-

Andy Buchannan loved his blades. He had a multitude of them. And he knew how to use them. In fact, he trained others how to use them. Not your normal fencing, though there was a touch of that in the instruction. Actually, he had developed his own techniques incorporating Far East Asian, Middle Eastern, European, and American West methods of using swords, long knives, and bowie knives.

It was only a sideline. Andy's main business was a law enforcement and military supplier of equipment, including firearms. He was equally adept at using the modern weapons as he was the ancient.

Fargo Thursten was probably Andy's most talented student. Fargo was also an in-law by marriage. Andy had married Cathy Abernathy and Fargo had married her twin sister Julie, just a few weeks later. The two men had similar interests and became good friends as well as brothers-in-law.

Where weaponry was Andy's forte, Fargo was an ATV and Dual Sport motorcycle fanatic. He owned a Big-Boys Toy Store, selling several lines of ATVs, UTVs, and motorcycles, along with accessories for them.

Cathy's and Julie's older brother Melvin was a camping enthusiast. Like his brothers-in-law, Melvin was in business associated with what he loved to do. He owned an outdoor equipment and supply business catering to wilderness and winter campers, re-enactors of several types, and several niche outdoor enthusiasts. His wife, Karen, was just as enthusiastic as Melvin and worked as a clerk in the store.

Andy's sister, Jo-An, was another member of the extended family. She was a doctor, specializing in Trauma Treatment. She was married to an Herbalist, Nathan Snyder. Nathan wasn't making a living as an Herbalist. He made his money playing the precious metals markets. Jo-An's younger cousin, Leslie Hamilton, stayed with Nathan and Jo-An. She'd just started medical school.

Then there were the "kids". Andy and Cathy's oldest, Matthew, sixteen, and youngest, Tess, fifteen. Casper, also fifteen, was Fargo's and Julie's only child.

They were a close knit family, with one overriding common interest. All four family groups were preppers. Andy was the eldest and had been prepping since a teen ager and was well into the self-sufficient lifestyle before he met any of the others. As the family came together and grew, each new member was brought into the fold.

The other three families had bought in on the same small working farm that Andy had purchased an interest in as his first major investment after starting the LE/Mil supply business. The farm was now fully owned by the four interrelated families. There was a resident manager in charge, with three permanent hands to work the farm.

The farm made little or no profit most years, but produced eighty-five percent of the food requirements for the four families, farm manger's family, and the hands' families, with enough left over to sell to the local stores in amounts that paid the expenses of running the farm.

With well-equipped and supplied individual homes, everyone planned to stay at home, or Bug-In, for most potential disasters. But some things called for bugging out to the Farm. There was only one hitch in their plans to bug-out. You sort of couldn't get from their homes to the Farm. At least not easily. There were several major obstacles between them. Two rivers, a small mountain range, and a large city. That meant they had to go somewhere else before they could head for the Farm.

It was a long way around using their Bug-out vehicles. But it was doable. There was a shorter route, but it meant leaving the road vehicles stashed and camouflaged, and heading cross country. There were a series of hiking, horse, and ATV trails through the mountains that could be used if the roads weren't passable. There were quite a few situations that would prevent the road vehicles from making it the long way around.

So, when the announcement came over the NOAA weather radio that a potential terrorist attack could leave the city, among many others, in ruins, the family decided to head for the farm. And perhaps half of the people in the area decided to head for the hills, literally, whether or not they had a place to go. They just wanted away from the city.

When Andy used the Low Band Business Band radios that all the families' were equipped with to announce the Bug-Out, everyone headed, per the plan, to Andy's store. They were all there within half an hour.

"Okay, everyone," Andy said when the families had gathered in the now locked down store. "Things have changed."

"Looking more like a general attack, now," chimed in Melvin. "Heard it coming over."

"Exactly," Andy replied. "And that changes things for us. Originally I thought we could just head out and take our time. Probably nothing will come of the terrorist attack, if there is one. But if there is a chance of all out nuclear war, I think we'd better continue with that in mind. Which means getting to the Farm as quickly as possible."

"Leave our homes behind?" asked Leslie.

A couple of people chuckled and Leslie blushed. "You know what I mean. Can't we stay and ride it out here?"

"No," Andy said carefully, not wanting to hurt Leslie's feelings. "Two reasons. One, our long term supplies are at the Farm. We'd have to go there eventually if this war talk is correct. And two, the Farm is going to need everyone there to protect it and what it contains. If we don't go there now, there might not be anything there to go to, later."

"I understand," Leslie said, sounding resigned.

"Should we chance the roads?" asked Fargo, "Or go ahead and plan on going cross country?"

Nathan was shaking his head. "When I came over the Interstate was already jammed. It could take us days to go around the long way."

"Be a lot easier and we can take a lot more, if we use the vehicles," Melvin said.

"True," Andy said. "But considering all the possibilities, I think we need to go home, secure the homes for long term absence, and then go directly to the mountain. Everyone okay with that?"

There was some minor discussion within the family units for a few seconds, but everyone agreed in the end. "Okay. Everyone take off and meet back here in three hours or less."

There was an eerie silence as the others left the store, leaving Andy, Cathy, Mathew, and Jess to discuss what they were going to do to get ready. "Cathy," Andy said, "You take the kids and go secure the house. Lock it down tight. There are some things I want to take care of here before we leave."

"Okay," Cathy replied. "Come on kids. The sooner we get this done the sooner we are on our way. I don't trust the government to give us word on when, or even if, the missiles are launched."

Pale, but showing the family trait of being game and ready to tackle anything, Mathew and Jess followed their mother toward the door of the store.

"You guys be careful," said Andy, following them to the door to relock it. "It's going to get crazy out there."

"Already is," said a man that just came up as Cathy and the teens left. "I need to get a few guns," he said to Andy.

"Sorry. We're closed."

Andy noticed the somewhat twisted smile on the man's face and was reaching for the Cold Steel Dragonfly O-Tanto sheathed behind his back even as the man drew a gun from his pocket. "I said I'm here to get some guns."

It was all one motion as Andy spun, pulled the O-Tanto and slid the point between the man's ribs, his left hand deflecting the gun. The gun went off, but the bullet flew wide, burying itself in the far wall behind Andy.

It took a solid tug to pull the fifteen-inch blade from the man's dead body. The sharp point had found the man's heart and he'd died before he could fall to the ground. Andy took a quick look around and then dragged the body into the store, over to one side of the door. He locked the front door again and then hurried to get done what he needed to do before he left.

He was waiting impatiently two and a half hours later, the work done and things laid out carefully on the various counters in the store. Everything he wanted protected that he couldn't take was in the vault. There were still quite a few things on the shelves, but none of them could be used against the Families.

Jo-An and Nathan, with Leslie, were the first to return. Andy had a Sig 226 .357 Sig in his hand when he went to the door to let them in. There were three other people wanting to get in. The Sig dissuaded them from trying. And, perhaps, the sight of the blood on the floor from the first attempt. Not to mention the firearms and blades that the three family members wore with confidence.

"Ewww!" Leslie said, seeing the blood and then the dead man.

"Trouble?" Nathan asked.

"None I couldn't handle," replied Andy. "You guys ready?"

"Yeah. We the first back?"

Andy nodded. "Got some stuff I want to take to keep it from getting into the wrong hands. Follow me."

Nathan let out a low whistle when he saw the things on the counters.

"Order for the Sheriff's Department just came in this morning," Andy explained, handing things to the three. "Patriot Ordnance Factory P416-7 .223 AR style PDWs. 7" barrels, select fire, with Redi-Mag carrier. Two C-Products 40-round magazines on the gun. Got FMCO vests set up for eight 40-round magazines. Unfortunately, the new body armor order is delayed, or I'd be handing them out, too.

Andy handed Jo-An and Leslie the PDWs. He picked up another gun and handed it to Nathan. "Another POF weapon," he explained. "P308-16.5 select-fire .308 rifle. 25-round magazine in the weapon and eight in the vests."

"I didn't think you liked the AR platform," Nathan said, checking the rifle the same way his wife and niece were checking the PDWs.

"Don't. Especially in .223. But these are the exception."

"I like it," Leslie said, slipping the magazine back into the PDW. She set it down and put on the vest. "All loaded up. Heavy."

"Yeah. I equipped them all the same. You can switch to your other gear if you want, but I thought these would give us interoperability. I'm beginning to think we're going to have some trouble getting out of town."

There was a banging on the door and Andy went to answer it. Jo-An, Nathan, and Leslie all took up defensive positions, and Andy had the 226 in hand when he opened the door. "Open up!" came a shout from outside when someone saw Andy approaching the door from inside.

"Closed!" Andy yelled through the door. He lunged back when someone outside fired a shotgun at him, expecting the birdshot to blow through the door. But all the windows in the store were armored glass. Some of the birdshot stuck in the outer face of the thick glass, but none even came close to penetrating.

Suddenly more shots rang out and the three men outside took off running. Fargo, Julie, and Casper were at the door, guns in hand. Andy let them in and quickly locked the door again.

"Getting wild out there," Fargo said. He saw the others with their new weapons and glanced at Andy.

"I've got some for you, too," Andy said, seeing the look.

"I'm pretty happy with what I have," Fargo said.

"Yeah. Take a look at these." Andy began handing out the Patriot Ordnance Factory guns to the Thursten's. A .308 rifle to Fargo and .223 PDWs to Julie and Casper.

"Wow!" Casper said, "Full auto!"

"And you know how to not use it if it isn't necessary," Fargo said. He was checking out the 16.5" barreled .308 rifle. The iron sights were folded down and a Bushnell Elite 4200 2.5-10x40mm scope on QD mount was in place.

Andy pointed to the ATN Otis-17 night vision scope that could quickly replace the Bushnell for night time. The PDWs were similarly equipped, only with an ATN Ultra Digital reflex sight instead of the Bushnell. An Otis-17 was available for each one of them, too.

"You rob a bank?" Fargo asked. He seemed satisfied with the rifle.

"Sheriff's department. They just came in. Didn't have a chance to call them. I'd rather have them in our hands than take a chance of them falling into someone else's."

"Good point." Fargo turned around. Leslie was watching the door and said, "It's Cathy, Mathew, and Jess. Hurry. There's some others out there that look like they want in."

When Andy opened the door, Fargo was right there with the rifle to his shoulder. Those following Cathy and the teens shrank back."

"Any sign of Melvin and Karen?" Cathy asked.

"Here they come." It was Leslie again.

This time Fargo had to shoot over the heads of the mob that was forming outside the store to keep them back so the Abernathy's could get inside.

Andy quickly distributed the rest of the eight PDWs and four P308s. Quick explanations, and some switching around of gear and the twelve family members got ready to leave. "I'm going to leave the door open," Andy said when the group was ready.

"But everything else…" Casper said, looking around at the shelves.

"Nothing I don't mind losing," Andy said. "It should distract those outside so we can leave with the fewest hassles possible."

"Oh. Okay. I just noticed there aren't any guns or ammo or anything. Just some clothes and camping gear and stuff."

"Yep," Andy said. "Everyone ready?" When the nods came, Andy unlocked the door and Fargo led the way out of the store, the rest moving close behind him. There were a few people around the locked vehicles, but when Andy called out, "It's all yours!" and pointed to the open door, the three different groups headed inside, just as Andy thought they would.

He thought he heard gunshots as he was pulling away from the store, the big one-ton Dodge diesel crew cab pickup bellowing slightly as he tromped the accelerator. He wanted to be long gone before the mob discovered there wasn't much useful left in the store.

Melvin, in a three-quarter ton Suburban, was next in line with Karen, followed by Nathan, Jo-An, and Leslie in their Suburban, with Fargo, Julie, and Casper bringing up the rear in a Ford three quarter ton crew cab pickup truck. All four pulled identical trailers loaded to the gills with ATVs, motorcycles, and gear.

It took quite a while to get to the point where they would leave the road vehicles and switch to the off-road gear. The going got rough at the end, but the trucks and SUVs made it, with the trailers. They parked in the midst of tall brush. It was unlikely anyone would be looking for vehicles in the spot, but after the trailers were unloaded, the rigs were covered with camouflage tarps and brush thrown over them in a random pattern.

"Okay. Listen up, everyone," Andy said after the trailers were unloaded. "We should be okay for a bit. Until we hit the first fire road. From there on, we could run into people. And they are going to be desperate people. Anything could happen.

"We are not going to take chances. We go armed at all times, and keep a sharp lookout. We avoid any and all confrontations we can. When we can't, we hit the problem with everything we have. It'll take a couple of days to get there. More if we have to take alternate routes because of dangerous situations.

"Now, we'll travel in the same order as we came up here, except the kids will be between Melvin and Karen, and Nathan and Jo-An."

"Shouldn't I ride point?" Mathew asked.

"Thanks, Mathew," Fargo said quickly. "But for the moment, we'd better let your Dad take the lead. He knows this end of this trail better."

"Yes, Son," Andy added. "I have a feeling you'll have more than one chance to take point."

"Okay," said the 16-year old. "I'll do whatever is best for the group."

"We all will," said Leslie. She had no wish to take point or tail end Charlie, but would if asked. She'd trained with the families for such a need.

Jess and Casper both stayed silent. There was no way any of the adults or Mathew would let them take any unnecessary risks. They'd be in the middle most, if not all, of the time.

After a few minutes to gear up, getting helmets, radios, gloves and LBE on and adjusted, they were ready to go. Andy climbed aboard the Bombardier Can-Am Outlander Max ATV. It was well equipped with cargo bags. Cathy got on behind him and gripped the passenger handles firmly. Without a word, Andy pulled away, checking the ride of the loaded MIG tent trailer hitched to the back of the Outlander.

Melvin and Karen were next, on a Suzuki V-Strom 1000cc dual sport bike. It too was outfitted with a set of cargo bags and had a trailer. A

Bunkhouse Lil'B motorcycle tent trailer, also loaded with supplies and gear.

Following them, spaced evenly apart, came Mathew, Jess, Casper, and Leslie, on identical Suzuki V-Strom 650 ABS dual sports. Like the bigger bikes, each one carried cargo bags loaded with supplies.

Nathan and Jo-An were also on a Suzuki V-Strom 1000cc dual sport bike, equipped nearly identically as Melvin and Karen's. Taking up the tail end Charlie position were Fargo and Julie, on a rig the same as Andy and Cathy's. Another Outlander Max ATV with MIG trailer.

Unlike many bikes and ATVs used in the wild, all of the families' vehicles were equipped with extra quite mufflers. They could be heard, of course, especially if really wound up, but for the most part, the group was about as quiet as a group of six motorcycles and two ATVs could be.

Andy set a good pace. Slow enough for the trailers to ride easily, but fast enough to get some distance behind them. There was little chatter among the group. Each had a Rider Link ORV-1 communication system in their helmets which allowed communication between rider and passenger on the two place rigs, and intercommunication between all the rigs using Dakota Alert M538HT MURS radios connected to the ORV-1 systems. Motorola HT-750 low band business band handy-talkies would be substituted for the MURS radios if the group separated and needed longer distance communications.

It was nearing dark when Andy pulled off the trail into an opening in the forest. The others followed, spacing the rigs out in a circle, just like the wagon trains of the western expansion.

Off came the helmets. "Mathew," Andy said, "I want you to run up the trail for a half mile or so. That should be where we intersect the fire road. Get close enough to see if anyone is about, but don't be seen."

"Okay, Dad," Mathew said eagerly as he put the helmet back on.

"You want us to start setting up camp?" Leslie asked.

"Let's wait for Mathew's scouting report. "Might go ahead and get a latrine ready."

"Okay," replied the young woman. She started to unsling the P416-7 but Andy spoke up.

"Better you keep it with you all the time, for the time being."

Leslie nodded, slinging the gun into a more comfortable position.

"I'll go with you, Leslie," Jess said. "I need to go."

The two had become close since Leslie had moved in with Jo-An and Nathan to attend the local medical school.

Casper went off in another direction to set up the men's latrine, e-tool in hand. An experienced camper, he knew exactly what to do.

Adult eyes drifted toward the narrow trail as they talked softly among themselves, discussing the possibilities that they might encounter. All breathed a sigh of relief when Mathew eased the Suzuki back into the open area quietly.

"Fire road is there, just where you said, Dad. Saw only one person. I feel bad. The guy only had a day pack on him and was wearing city clothes. He might have a rough time of it tonight if it gets as cold as the forecast this morning said it will."

All eyes were on Andy. "He's on his own, unless he hooks up with someone else on the road. We can't take in and care for every person we see."

"I understand, Dad," Mathew said softly. "It was just... hard... to not lend a hand."

"You did the right thing," Andy replied. "There are going to be many hard decisions made over the next few weeks and perhaps months. I'm not saying we won't ever help anyone, but we are going to have to be very selective about who we do help and who we don't. Let's go ahead and get camp set up."

The sounds of setting up the tent trailers, and the two separate tents the teens would use were subdued, as the group practiced strict sound discipline. It wasn't long before hot water was available to rehydrate the Mountain House campers' meals that would be everyone's supper, with tea, coffee, or hot chocolate afterwards with a handful of gorp for desert.

Andy hesitated for a moment as everyone got ready to go to bed, but after a few seconds said, "You have the first watch, Mathew. Leslie, you're next. I'll take the third. Fargo? Melvin? Nathan?"

"I'll take the last watch," Melvin said immediately.

Andy nodded, and group paired off, going to their tent trailers, with Mathew and Casper sharing one on-the-ground tent, and Leslie and Jess another. Mathew put his gear inside the tent, and then went back to the spot that had been picked out for the sentries to be during the night.

A stressful day and a tiring one, the occasional gunshot heard during the night kept everyone from sleeping all that well, except for Jess and Casper.

Melvin had hot water ready the next morning when Andy got up just before dawn. The two talked quietly over cups of coffee as they waited a bit longer to wake the others. But the wakeups weren't needed. Even Jess and Casper were up and about shortly after first light.

Everyone was in a heavy sweater or light jacket for breakfast. The temperature had dropped significantly during the night. Breakfast went quickly and the group was ready to get back on the trail by the time the sun began to warm the mountain slightly.

Again Andy led the way. He was keeping a close eye on the GPS navigation system installed on the Outlander Max. When he was sure he was a few yards away from the fire road he stopped and keyed the M538HT and spoke into the boom microphone in his helmet. "Give it a look, Mathew."

Andy felt Cathy touch his shoulder in question. Through the intercom he told his wife, "He'll be okay. Mathew took to the training like a duck to water. He knows what to do and how to do it."

"I know, Honey. But these times now…"

"We just have to depend on the fact that we raised and taught him well."

Cathy leaned forward and put her arms around Andy, pressing against his back.

Mathew went past on the Suzuki V-Strom 650 ABS slowly and quietly. He was still in sight when he stopped and got off the back. He disappeared from sight for what seemed an eternity to Cathy, but he was suddenly on the radio and sounded just fine to her.

"Fire road is here okay. But there are half a dozen people camping right at the junction. And they have guns aplenty. Mostly hunting rifles and shotguns though."

"Ease on back here," Andy transmitted. "We need to palaver."

When Mathew made it back, Nathan gestured to Leslie and she and Mathew took up watch positions for the group as the adults got together to discuss options. It didn't take long.

They would avoid the group currently on the fire road.

"Mathew, go back and keep an eye on the group. Leslie, go look for a path the Outlanders can take to intersect the fire road to the west. Start back at that opening about a quarter mile back. The rest of us will wait here until we hear from you."

Her eyes wide, Leslie looked at Nathan and Jo-An. Jo-An gave a slight nod.

"You can do it, Leslie," Jess said reassuringly.

Still a bit unsure, Leslie turned the bike around and headed back down the track they'd come up. It was some time before Leslie reported in by radio. "Okay. I think I found a route. I blazed it as I traveled. I was afraid I wouldn't be able to find it again, once I did find it. Orange survey tape. Little pieces, so look carefully."

"Good work, Leslie," Andy said. "Ease on back, Mathew. Keep an eye on the back trail. Pull the blazes as you come. We're heading out now." With that, Andy started the Outlander Max and headed back down the trail, the others following closely."

When they were all together again, just off the fire road, Mathew handed Leslie a handful of survey tape pieces. She stuffed them in a pocket for use later, if needed.

The families had an easy run for almost an hour. Andy suddenly stopped in the middle of the fire road. "Something is wrong," he said over the radio. "Mathew?"

"I'm on it, Dad."

"Be careful, Son," Andy said quietly. "This could be a problem."

"Will do." Mathew passed those ahead of him and then slowed down as he continued up the fire road. He went around a curve and Andy felt himself tense. When it came, it was a shock, even to Andy, who half expected it.

The sudden gunfire was loud and intense.

"Andy?" Cathy asked, clutching her husband in fear for her oldest child.

"Ambush! Ambush!" Mathew's voice was loud in the helmet speakers of all the family members.

Andy recognized the sound of Mathew's P416-7 on full auto. Even as he ordered the others to leave the vehicles and take cover in the forest on each side of the fire road, Andy admired the short, even bursts of fire his son was using.

A few seconds later, the PDW slung down his chest, Mathew came charging back on the Suzuki to join the others. He stopped the bike and took up a position in the forest. He was breathing hard, but sounded calm when he said, "About fifteen or twenty. Not sure. But they have a lot of guns. Not just hunting guns, this time."

"Andy?" asked Fargo.

Andy didn't have a chance to respond. The group was after Mathew. At least ten came running around the corner of the fire road thirty yards ahead the families. He began to fire the P308-16.5 .308 rifle.

The rest of the family joined in. All were in prone positions, behind the nearest big tree. There was a tremendous amount of noise for a few seconds as full auto fire from the PDWs raked the approaching group. Andy, Fargo, Melvin, and Nathan were picking off individuals with the most dangerous weapons with single shots.

A second, much smaller group, came around the bend, this time more cautiously and not in the middle of the road. They were working their way up in the edges of the forest flanking the fire road.

With controlled bursts from the .223s and single shots from the .308s soon had those that were still alive hurrying back around the bend.

"Fargo! Melvin! On me!" Andy yelled and stood up. He began to advance up the fire road slowly, the rifle at the ready. As the other two kept an eye up the road, Andy checked each of the bodies, tossing weapons out of reach in case someone was faking their death.

Not all of those down were dead. There were moans and cries for help from three of them. None reached for the weapons as Andy moved them.

"Coup de grâce?" asked Melvin.

Andy shook his head. "I can't bring myself to do that. Keep an eye on them. Fargo and I'll check around the bend."

They found three more bodies of men that had managed to get back around the bend despite having been shot. There were no others in sight on the road or along the edges of the forest.

"What do you think, Andy? "High speed run, guns ready?"

"I think so. Let's get back."

"We taking the guns?"

Andy hesitated. "Yeah. I guess so. Don't want to leave them for someone else to use against us."

As they walked back toward their vehicles, Andy and Fargo began to collect the guns and accoutrements. Both men's hands were full and Melvin bent over to gather up those weapons near him.

"Better let us get them," Andy said.

Before the words were barely out of his mouth, one of the dead, that wasn't as dead as he'd seemed before, rolled over, raising a handgun as he did so. The man had Melvin cold.

It wasn't a conscious thought that had Andy dropping everything in his arms. With his rifle slung across his chest, his right hand automatically went to the hilt of the Cold Steel Dragonfly katana carried on his back under his pack.

One amazingly fast movement and the man on the ground screamed, his right hand, still with the pistol grasped in it, fell to the ground, severed completely just above the wrist. The screams stopped when Andy slid the point of the katana into the man's chest, slicing the heart open.

"Sweet Mercy!" Melvin said, face pale. "I thought I was a dead man." He was staring at the body on the ground, but then looked over at Andy. "Thanks, man. You saved my life."

"Slickest move I ever saw you make with a blade, buddy," Fargo said.

"Sorry, guys," Melvin said then. "I should have been more alert."

"Water under the bridge. Let's get these weapons secured, clear a path, and get on the trail again." Andy wiped the blood off the katana on the dead man's shirt before sheathing it again. He'd clean it thoroughly that night.

The rest of the family members came out of the forest when Andy called out the okay. "Good work, Son," he told Mathew. He turned to look at Jess. "You okay, Honey?"

"I never shot anybody before," she said softly. "I didn't like it."

Cathy hugged Jess against her. "That's good, Sweetheart. None of us like what just happened, but if we had not reacted the way we did, things would have been very much worse for us."

Jess nodded and pulled away from her mother. Everyone began to go over their respective vehicles, looking for damage from bullets. There were a couple of scars, and the windshield of Melvin's Suzuki had a tiny hole through it down low on the left side, but that was the limit of the damage. The group had mostly been shooting into the edge of the forest where the family members had taken cover.

"You want me on point?" Mathew asked as everyone began to get their helmets back on and climb aboard the rigs.

"Why don't I take his bike and run point," Fargo said. "He can ride with Julie."

Andy considered it. Fargo looked at him and shrugged slightly.

"I can do it, Dad," Mathew replied to Fargo's comment. He didn't look at his Uncle.

"Yes. Yes, you can. Go ahead. But I want you to keep a very close eye out and be even more cautious than you have been."

"I will. I'd much rather avoid a confrontation than be in one. I learned my lesson just now."

"Let's stay together until we get past their camp," Andy said as he started the Outlander Max. "Keep your weapons ready, every other one to the right, the rest to the left."

Mathew took the lead, and moved forward slowly, eyes darting right to left and back again, keeping the entire front 120° area under close scrutiny. There was no sign of the survivors of the group that had attacked them.

Andy had Mathew stop so Fargo could get off his Outlander Max and check the things the group had left behind at the ambush site. He shook his head at Andy, and the families moved

24

on, Mathew out in front by fifty yards, going slowly.

"Make a right up ahead," Andy told Mathew an hour later.

"Hold up, everyone," Mathew replied immediately. "Got another group up here. Right at the intersection, like before."

"Pull back. I want to look it over," Andy said. He stopped and got off the ATV.

With the helmet in Cathy's hands, and the POF .308 in his, Andy walked forward, meeting Mathew a few steps from the ATV. Mathew flipped the visor off his helmet up and said, "A big group. They have guns, too. But there are a bunch of women and children with them."

"Okay. I'll check it out. Have Fargo and Nathan come up and cover me."

Mathew wanted to protest, but followed his father's order after only a moment of hesitation. He spoke to his Uncles and then went back to the head of the column, his PDW at the ready.

Andy slung the POF down across his chest, but unsnapped the flap on the Sig 226 .357 Sig holster. The katana was still across his back, and the O-tanto hung from his belt on the left side. "Hello the camp!" he called out when he was in sight of them.

His eyes roved over the group. There were at least fifty people, and about a fourth of them were armed, with three of the gun holders being women. There several more women in the group, along with at least ten young children. Andy looked at the camp set up at the side of the fire road in an open area. Only six tents, two of them small solo campers' bivys.

Everyone with a gun had it leveled at Andy after he shouted. "Not here to hurt anyone or take anything," he said loudly. "Just want to move on through."

"We heard gunfire earlier. Was that you?"

Andy nodded and took a few steps forward. "A group tried to ambush us. They weren't successful."

"Stay right where you are," said the man that seemed to be in charge. Women and older children were herding the smaller children toward the tents, out of the line of fire, if trouble broke out.

"How many are you?" asked the man.

A woman called out, "Do you have any food and water to spare? We're in desperate need."

"There's a cree…" Andy started to tell them about the creek not too far away, but it was known to be infected with a couple of microorganisms and any water taken from it needed to be boiled or otherwise treated before drinking. Andy had doubts those of the group would take the time to do either.

"Yes. We can spare some water. And a bit of food for the little ones," Andy said. "But you get it after we pass through."

"What if we decide to just take it?" asked one of the men on the periphery of the group. He was of slight build, wore his hair in a short pony tail, and had a scraggly looking Van Dyke beard.

Several people told him to shut up, and the man in charge glared at him. "We don't want any trouble, mister. But we sure could use some help."

Andy lifted one of the MURS radios, identical to the ones mounted on the vehicles, and spoke into it. "Everyone come on through. Keep your guns pointed down to the ground. But be ready for anything. Real slow. I don't want any threatening moves."

A minute later Andy stepped out of the way and let Mathew go past him. "Hold up about three hundred yards out."

A spot opened up and Mathew drove through it, turning up the trail that intersected the one they were on. One by one the rest of the family members passed. All could feel the eyes of the refugees on them. When Julie was well up the other trail, Andy walked forward. "We'll be back in just a few minutes with some food and water."

The big guy, the one in charge, nodded. "Don't let us down. Please. Not much we can do about it, but we have some little ones here…"

"So I see. Just remember the food is for them. The water is for everyone. Get some containers ready. I don't want to give up any of ours. Oh. Do you have a destination in mind?"

The man sighed and shook his head. "I get some containers rounded up."

Andy hurried to join the family at the vehicles.

"Where's Uncle Melvin and Uncle Fargo?" asked Jess, looking back down the trail worriedly.

"They're keeping an eye on the group. So nothing bad happens. We're going to give the group some water, and food for the kids. Help your mother get a few things ready. As things were gathered up, Andy considered for a long time, but finally dug into one of the cargo bags and took out a Katadyn Hiker Pro water filter unit and a pair of spare filter cartridges for it.

"You going to give them your filter?" Nathan asked.

"Yeah," Andy replied. "Reluctantly. It's a third line spare. The water we're giving them won't last long, and the spring is contaminated. If they discover it and drink without treating the water, some of them are going to get sick, for sure."

Nathan nodded. "Just checking."

With Mathew and Leslie helping, Andy and Cathy carried the water containers and armfuls of food back down the trail to the group.

With most of the group gathered round, Andy transferred the water to the group's containers, while Cathy handed out the food to those that said they had children.

28

"What about us?" asked the obnoxious little guy.

"You'll just have to wait until you get where you're going," Andy replied coldly. He turned to the big guy and handed him the water filter. "Each filter is good for about 200 gallons. There's a small creek about two hundred yards that way," Andy said, pointing into the forest. "It is contaminated, but the filter will take out the harmful bacteria. Don't let anyone drink the unfiltered water. They will most likely get sick if they do. And you don't need that."

"Okay. Thanks. Why are you doing this? You could have just kept going."

"We decided it was just the right thing to do. Sorry it can't be more. But I won't risk my own people."

"Yeah. I understand. Thank you." The man didn't offer to shake hands, and neither did Andy.

Cathy looked back as the four of them moved back toward the vehicles. "We've done all we can do without serious jeopardy to our own children," Andy said softly.

"I know. It's just… Well… You know what it is…"

"Yeah. I'd like to take in everyone. But we can't. If this war happens, millions are going to die, if not billions. I don't want my family to be in that group."

"Nor I," replied Cathy, turning back resolutely to join her family.

Everything was repacked and ready to go a few minutes later when Melvin and Fargo appeared in the trail, having come through the forest to join them without being seen. It was Melvin that asked Andy, "You think that big guy knew Fargo and I were out there? He kept scanning the area where we were."

"Probably. And I think it is part of the reason nothing happened. It could easily have gone badly if the guy had started something he thought he could get by with."

"Yeah. Best we did it the way we did," Fargo said. He was putting on his helmet and getting ready to get on the Outlander Max with Julie.

With Mathew again in the lead a few hundred feet ahead, the families began travelling again. It was slower going. The Suzuki V-Strom 650 ABS bike had no trouble. Even the big V-Strom 1000s with trailer had no trouble with the trail.

The Outlander Maxes, with their larger, tandem wheel trailers had a few tight spots they had to maneuver through. But they were able to keep going without further incident until just before nightfall.

Mathew had stopped and waited for the rest at a suitable spot for camp. As it had the night before, everything went smoothly during their overnight stay.

There was a mixture of light rain and heavy snow the next morning when Andy started up one of the stoves to get water hot, having pulled the last shift of the night. Cathy came out of the trailer tent, but turned around and went back inside. When she came out the second time she had on a heavy coat with hood.

"Nasty out," she said when Andy handed her a cup of coffee.

That was the general consensus as the rest of the family members got up to face another day. But everyone had appropriate gear for the weather, and were bundled up nicely when they broke camp and headed on their way again. The rain had turned to sleet, with some snow. An hour later it was all snow falling. And it was falling fast and heavy.

This time when they stopped for a noon break, a couple of stoves were set up and water heated for hot drinks. The prior two days the noon stops had been quick, with only food bars, jerky, and gorp washed down with water. But Andy thought that a warming drink would cheer everyone's spirits a little. He knew it would his.

So coffee, tea, and hot chocolate were prepared and handed around after the same meal they'd had during the other lunches was finished. Afterwards, the family hit the road again, with Mathew still in the lead. He kept a slow pace, to allow the Outlanders Maxes ample time to negotiate the narrow trail.

"Something... Something ahead on the trail," Mathew said on the radio. He had come to a stop and let the others come up to him. "I can't tell what it is, but… I think it is a body."

"Check it out and then I'll take a look," Jo-An remarked.

"I have a feeling whoever it is won't be needing your expertise," Andy said. He was off the Outlander Max, having removed his helmet. He took the baseball cap Cathy handed him and put it on his head.

"Nathan, come on up and give me some cover." Before Mathew could offer, Andy spoke again. "I want you on the back trail now, Mathew. I was going to switch when we hit the next fire road, but we might as well make the change now. Stop occasionally and listen for anyone that might be following."

"Okay Dad." Mathew turned the Suzuki around and eased around the others, going far enough so he could hear, but where he could still see the rest.

Nathan was ready and moved into the edge of the forest, tracking Andy as he moved forward to check on the partially snow covered body a few yards up the trail. Even the first quick look told Andy the tale. It was the man in city clothes and day pack that Mathew had seen the first day.

"Remarkable that he made it this far," Andy said after motioning Nathan forward. Andy checked the body. It was stone cold. The man had been dead for quite some time. It was a struggle to search the man's body. He'd apparently worked up a sweat, probably by keeping moving when the temperature dropped. His wet clothes had frozen stiff.

But Andy was able to get the man's wallet and opened it up. "Stanton Jones. Born 1963." Andy handed the wallet to Nathan and then worked the daypack off Jones' stiff arms. Nathan saw Andy shake his head when he opened the pack.

Andy held it out so Nathan could look inside.

"Geez! He as much as killed himself," Nathan muttered. There were three empty 750mL bottles of Scotch in the pack. Even empty, they were carefully cushioned to protect them from breaking. A kitchen knife, can opener, spoon and fork were the only other things in the bag.

Andy started to toss the pack aside, but decided to hang onto it. Might be useful as a hand out at some point. The two men headed back to the others and the vehicles. Andy tossed the daypack up onto the top of the load on the MIG tent trailer.

Jo-An was watching the two and when she saw Nathan shake his head, she got back on the Suzuki V-Strom 1000, leaving room for Nathan to get on in front of her.

"You want me on point?" Leslie asked before Andy could let Melvin know he wanted him and Karen to take the lead.

Andy started to say no, but hesitated for a moment. She was offering, she was eighteen, and there shouldn't be too much else going on up this high. "Yeah. Take it slow and easy. And keep a sharp eye out for anything suspicious."

"Okay Uncle Andy." Leslie eased the Suzuki forward and pulled out into the lead, swinging well around the dead body. Andy followed, barely able to avoid clipping the frozen body.

For over an hour they continued to climb at a slow pace, the snow getting heavier and heavier. "There's a good spot to camp here," Leslie said in the late afternoon.

"Okay, Leslie. Check a little further up the trail and we'll pull in where you are." Andy had really wanted to top the high pass and get down a ways on the other side, but Leslie was about worn out. It was primarily her nervous energy being sapped, but it was energy, and a person only had so much. Better to let her get some rest and have everyone fresh when they started down the mountain.

"Uncle Andy," came Leslie's voice over the radio just as he turned into the open spot on the side of the trail. "I'm right at the top. Should we just go down now? Try to get out of the snow?"

Andy heard the fatigue in her voice and looked around at Jess and Casper. Both were leaning forward, resting their helmeted heads on their crossed arms atop the gas tank cargo bags. They, too, were showing their fatigue.

"No. Come on back. We'll camp here. Make the crossing in the morning."

Even with the snow still coming down, the experienced family had camp set up quickly. When Casper asked if they could have a fire, Andy and Fargo looked at one another for a moment. Fargo nodded and Andy told Casper. "Small one should be okay. You know the drill."

"Yes, Uncle Andy." Happy with the decision, Casper hurried to prove his skills in fire making in adverse conditions. Fargo kept an eye on him as he helped Julie set up the tent on the MIG trailer. But Casper was well trained. He had the small fire going in a short time, with plenty of additional wood ready to feed it.

"Watch the fire, Jess?" Casper asked his cousin. "I want to get a lot more wood."

"Okay, Casper. It feels nice. Thanks for making it."

"Sure thing," Casper replied. He headed off into the forest with his tomahawk, to bring in more branches off the leaning and standing deadfall timber the forest was peppered with.

No one was inclined to stay up after full dark, despite the fire. Casper carefully banked the fire, so it would be ready the next morning. Andy, Melvin, Fargo, and Nathan took the night watches, after convincing the wives that they'd have plenty to do in the future.

Nathan had the fire going when the others crawled out of the tents the next morning. The snow had stopped, and light was showing through the tops of the trees. But it was much colder than the previous evening.

The men stood around, eating their Mountain House breakfasts, discussing the situation. "What do you think, Andy? Push on, or lay up a day and let some of the snow disappear. It should warm up late this afternoon, according to the last forecast I heard." Fargo took a swig of coffee and then began to eat again.

Andy looked at the other two. "What do you think guys?"

"I'd rather get where we're going, Melvin said. "As long as you think the kids can make it on their bikes. It's going to be a struggle, but I think Nathan and I will be okay on the big bikes, even with the trailers."

"I don't know," Nathan said. "Speaking as Devil's Advocate, wouldn't it be better to wait and see? Might not even have to continue if the situation stabilizes. I've been listening to the shortwave every night. Nothing has happened yet."

Andy looked away, seeming to study the bright light as the sun climbed behind the trees. "I think we'd better push on. We know what is behind us. I don't want to run into any of the people we've already had encounters with. And even if this situation does taper off, we might as well use it as an exercise."

It was enough to convince the others. Andy was the leader of the family for a reason. All the others knew he took everything he could think of into account before he made a difficult decision.

Casper made sure the fire was out and could not reignite and spread, then forked his Suzuki and started it. Leslie went ahead and pulled forward, without waiting to be told, and Mathew waited for the others to get almost out of sight before he began to follow, stopping from time to time, just as he had the day before, to take off his helmet and listen. In the cold, crisp air, sound would travel far, even in the forest.

As they topped the pass, Leslie pulled over in the first wide spot on the trail and let the others come up to her. "Is that the farm?" she asked, pointing toward the distant flatlands.

"Sure is," Nathan said. "Can't mistake those five big blue silos, even at this distance."

"Means we're almost there," Jess said, straining upwards slightly so she could see over the tops of the nearest trees.

"Well, closer than we were," Cathy replied. "Still a long way to go."

She looked over at Andy and Fargo. They had their heads together, looking off slightly away from the line of sight to the farm.

"What's the matter?" she asked, going over to them. All the others turned to see what was happening.

"Smoke," Fargo replied, pointing to the very faint, rising column of smoke. It was hard to see and dissipated quickly.

"Oh. Is it on our route?" Cathy asked.

"Depends on the route we take," Andy said. "It is on the route I intended to take. If we swing wide, we'll avoid them. But it will add half a day to the trip."

"Not everyone can be an enemy."

"True, Cathy," Andy said. "But right now, I'd just as soon not have any friends on the route, either."

A few seconds of silence and then Andy said, "We take the long way. Might be worse, but we'll never know for sure. Leslie, we pick up a really old and overgrown fire road ahead. Bear right when it splits."

"Okay, Uncle Andy."

Everyone put their helmet back on and Leslie led the way again. The travelling was much easier once they hit the fire road. Even though it was overgrown to a degree, it was wider than the other trail and much easier for the ATVs and bikes to traverse. And there wasn't nearly as much snow on this side of the mountain. They ran out of it just before noon.

All took advantage of the noon break to re-layer their clothing for the warmer temperatures on this side of the mountain, already down lower than they'd been the day before.

They had not travelled far after they ate when there was a loud squeal in the helmet speakers. Andy called for a halt. "Everyone gather round."

There were questions all around about if anyone else had heard the squeal. "I think we just got hit with an EMP," Andy said. "And the GPS lost all the satellites that are in view. I think someone has either taken them off-line or destroyed them. Either way, it is bad news. Everyone's rig doing okay? EMP didn't affect them?"

"I told you it wouldn't," Nathan said. "The electronics just don't have all that much wiring leading into them. Same with the MURS radios. The antennas are too short for them to get much of a pulse."

"Well," Fargo said, "If Andy is right, and you are right, as it seems both of you are, we're getting off lucky. But it also means a nuclear exchange is very, very likely. We need to get to the farm post haste."

"Right," Andy said. He took a topographic map out of the fuel tank pouch and unfolded it. "This is the route we'll take down." He pointed out the way points where they would change direction or switch from one trail to another, marking each one on the plastic overlay.

"Cathy, you'll have to do the navigating for me. Give me a head's up when a turn is coming up."

Cathy nodded and took the map. She studied it and the surrounding area as Andy continued.

"Okay. We're going to change up the convoy order a little. Leslie, I want you and Mathew to stay close on the back end. Casper and Jess still in the middle. But I'll lead, with Fargo behind me. I want to move quickly but still cautiously. We could be in the middle of a nuclear war in hours. Minutes, perhaps."

It wasn't only the teens that had white faces when Andy stopped talking. And it was worse a few moments later when a brilliant flash lighted the already sunny sky. All eyes turned toward the source. It was behind them, to the north, and well east of their position.

"That tears it," Andy said urgently. "People are going to be desperate and wild. Make sure your weapons are loaded and ready. We're going to be moving fast. If I miss the signs of an ambush, and we get caught in one, spray and pray and keep going as fast as you can to get out of the killing zone.

"It isn't likely, as I doubt anyone will be expecting someone to be coming down off the mountain. But there may be individuals like we ran into before that will shoot before asking questions. But bear in mind that we fire only if fired upon. Unless, of course, the situation dictates otherwise.

"Everyone go to the bathroom. We'll top off the fuel tanks from our cans. We won't be stopping for a long time."

It was a quiet, subdued group that went about getting ready for the hard run down the mountain. It took only a few minutes to get ready, but in that time, another flash had brightened the sky, this one in the far distance, but again well east of the farm. This one they could see the mushroom cloud or the top of it anyway, as it climbed above the distant horizon.

Andy checked behind him one last time and then they were off. The tandem wheeled MIG trailers rode a bit better than the smaller and lighter Lil'Bs behind the Suzuki V-Strom 1000s, but everyone was an experienced rider and Andy was able to keep the speed up.

They were on a more travelled fire road in less than an hour and Andy was able to pick up more speed. The southern side of the mountain was steeper, and the valley floor was at a higher elevation than that on the north side, so the trip was shorter, despite some of the trails zigzagging due to the steepness, than the trip up.

It wasn't until they were on the home stretch down the mountain, on a steep fire road that angled just slightly across the base of the mountain that they ran into the first panicked people. They were fleeing from their now EMP disabled vehicles, left sitting on the interstate that ran around the base of the mountain.

The man in the lead of a group of ten people stopped in the middle of the trail and began waving his arms when he saw the first ATV approaching. Andy slowed down, but he didn't stop. The man jumped out of the way at the last second and the convoy sped between the members of the group as it split toward each side of the fire road.

There was a lot of yelling and screaming, and one person tried to grab Mathew from his bike as he was passing. But Mathew kicked the man away, hardly slowing down as he did so. That was the first bunch. There were several more, the lower down the mountain they went.

Jess sounded like she was crying when she suddenly asked over the radio, "Why are all these people coming up here? Why aren't they trying to get to shelter?"

Cathy spoke soothingly to her daughter. "People panic, Sweetheart. They aren't thinking rationally. Just reacting wildly to the fact we are in the middle of a nuclear war."

"But they are going to die up there!"

"Yes. Perhaps most of them," Andy said. "But there is nothing we can do to help them."

"Okay," Jess said, sobbing slightly. But she never faulted on the bike, maintaining position and speed.

It wasn't until just before hitting the county road where the fire road they were on connected to the highway system, that they ran into trouble. A group of at least a hundred people were spread out along the trail, taking up the entire width.

Andy slowed and stopped several yards from the people in the lead. "Clear the way! We're coming through!" he yelled through the opening of his helmet after he lifted the visor.

"No way!" someone screamed. "Give us those rigs! We're going up the mountain, not down!"

"Fire a burst over their heads, Cathy," Andy said, flipping the helmet visor back down.

"Andy?" Cathy asked.

But her husband just said, "Do it."

Swinging the P416-7 clear of Andy's body, and tensioning it from her shoulder with the sling, Cathy triggered a short burst well over the heads of the group. The reaction was immediate. Screaming in fear, the majority of those in front of them dived for the concealment of the forest. A couple of people stood their ground. And very foolishly drew weapons, bringing them up to fire on the convoy.

Cathy didn't hesitate. Her babies came first. She fired a long burst, this time directly at the three people beginning to aim guns at Andy. The burst was effective in getting the three to dive away, forgetting about their guns, despite only nicking one of them. But that was all the damage that was done as the gun, held one handed, even with the tension of the sling, climbed high to the right, all but one round pelting the forest well down the trail.

Andy gunned the Outlander Max, but only pulled over to one side of the road. "Go! Go! Go!" he shouted into the radio. He lifted the POF .308 rifle and began to fire over the heads of anyone that showed one, as the rest of the family rode past at high speed.

Julie, Karen, and Jo-An all had their carbines up and were firing short bursts to each side of the fire road as they traveled between the split group. As soon as Mathew and Leslie went by, Andy dropped the rifle, letting the sling catch and hold it against his chest.

He saw Mathew suddenly wobble, but Mathew didn't go down, horsing the bike back onto course. Andy accelerated and drew as close as he dared to the rear of Mathew's Suzuki.

"Oh, No!" Cathy cried out. "He's been shot!"

"I'm okay," Mathew said, keying the radio. "Just my shoulder. I'll be okay. We can't stop."

After an agonizing period of time, at least for Andy and Cathy, Fargo finally slowed down, and those following did the same. They circled the vehicles and everyone except Cathy and Jo-An had their weapons up, keeping watch around the circle. Cathy and Jo-An were with Mathew. He'd sat down heavily on the ground after stopping the bike.

The two women struggled to get his bike jacket off, and then his shirt and undershirt. "It doesn't look too bad," Jo-An said, opening her medical bag. It was more to reassure Cathy than Mathew.

"How is he?" Andy called over his shoulder.

"He'll be all right," Jo-An reassured Andy. "Bullet was a through and through, front to back, just under his armpit. Going to be sore, but he should heal without any problems. Barring the unforeseen."

Another couple of minutes and Jo-An had the entrance and exit holes bandaged. She gave Mathew the first pill in a cycle of antibiotics to lessen the chance of infection, and a pain killer to reduce the pain that Mathew was just starting to feel.

"I'm okay. We can get back on the road," Mathew said, climbing slowly to his feet. He reached for his bike but Andy was there.

"Hold it sport. You're riding with your mother. I'll take the bike."

"But I…"

Andy didn't have to say anything else. Mathew knew the look his father was giving him. No arguments accepted. "Okay. Mom, you want me to drive?"

"No, Mathew. You just ride quietly."

All eyes turned to the south suddenly. The sound of gunfire was faint, but hearable. "That could be at the farm," Fargo said, looking quickly at Andy.

"Yes, it could," Andy replied. He took out his Motorola HT-750 from the gear on the ATV and keyed it up, all the while looking toward the horizon where the farm was.

"We're about twelve miles out. We hear gunfire, Brandon. Is that you?"

Those close enough heard Brandon's reply. "Yes. We're under siege! That lousy pumpkin head Alfred brought a bunch of his buddies with him. They're trying to take the farm."

"We'll be there as soon as we can," Andy said and put the handheld back into the fuel tank bag. "We'll scope it out when we get closer. Let's go."

A few seconds later and the group was on the road again. Though they met a few people on the road on the way to the Interstate, none presented any trouble, though several people did try to get them to stop. But Andy, on Mathew's Suzuki V-Strom 650 ABS, riding in the lead, just drove around them and the rest of the family followed.

After crossing under the Interstate they didn't see anyone else until they got close to the farm. Then it was only the backs of men crouched behind a couple of pickups. One would pop up and fire a shot and then drop back down.

As soon as he saw them, Andy stopped the convoy at a small copse bordering the road. "Okay. Jo-An, you're in charge here with Leslie, Mathew, Jess, and Casper."

That look was on Andy's face again when Mathew started to speak up in protest. But he held his peace. His father wasn't going to let him join the fight. Not unless it came this way. He nodded at his father.

"Cathy, I want you and Karen on the Outlanders after we disconnect the trailers. With Karen riding behind one of you so she can provide cover fire. You'll be our rescue team in case one of us goes down.

"Fargo, you and I go in directly. Melvin, Nathan, you two keep our flanks clear once they figure out we're here. You guys ready?"

There were nods all around. All knew the price they might be paying to keep the farm in the family, but the cost of not doing so could be much worse. Even Casper and Jess understood and were checking their PDWs just in case the fight came to them.

With magazines topped off and equipment checked and ready, the four men of the family began a slow advance, using all the concealment that was available, and what cover there was. Melvin and Nathan began to swing away to each side as Andy and Fargo approached the two pickup trucks and the men hiding, they thought, behind them.

Andy simply could not bring himself to start shooting at the men's backs. Fargo looked at him when Andy hesitated, and then nodded, bringing the POF .308 rifle up to his shoulder.

"Hey!" Andy yelled. "Drop the guns and you'll…"

Andy didn't have a chance to complete the sentence. All four men began to turn around, bringing their guns up. One triggered a shot well before his gun was on line. It was enough for Andy and Fargo. Both let loose with quick bursts, taking all four men down in only fractions of a second.

Hurrying forward to kick the guns away from the fallen attackers, Andy and Fargo crouched behind the truck. Andy took out the HT-750 and contacted Brandon. "We took four out at the pickups. What else is going on?"

Andy had to hold the radio close to his ear when Brandon answered. A long volley of more than two dozen shots sounded as the rest of the attackers fired on the fortifications of the farm. They still didn't know they'd lost four people.

Slipping the radio back into a pocket, Andy leaned forward and said, "They have the place surrounded. Went over the back fence apparently and got inside the yard, but they're pinned down from the house. You go around the other way and I'll go this. Take Nathan and see if you can get into position to cover us when Melvin and I open up on them from the fence line."

"Okay bro. You be careful."

"You too, man."

Each man nodded at the other and then turned to go in opposite directions. Fargo made it to where Nathan was and they began working their careful way around the corner of the property. One of Alfred's men spotted Fargo and realized that the four men in the front of the house were out of action. He fired several shots. Andy went from the crouch he was in to prone as Melvin cut loose with a short burst to keep the man's head down.

The two men with the one that had fired had to shift positions to avoid Melvin's fire, but that put them in sight of the house. Both were quickly taken down, leaving only the first man. He threw down his gun and raised his hands, shouting, "I give up! I give up!"

Andy muttered under his breath. He should have shot a moment before. Prisoners complicated things. "Melvin, make sure he's secured," Andy said, as they both moved forward to the man."

Andy signaled the house that the position was secure as Melvin took some 550 cord from his vest and hog tied the prisoner. "Man! That's too tight!" complained the man lying face down on the ground.

"You'd better just be glad we don't shoot prisoners," Andy said over his shoulder. "At least, not yet," he added softly.

Andy had scoped out the situation in the back yard. Five men were in various spots of concealment, using what little cover was available to them to best advantage. They were well protected from the house, but various parts of anatomy were exposed to Andy and Melvin.

"Okay, Melvin. We're going to have to go in hot and heavy. Alfred knows the defenses well enough to take good advantage of them. We either have to get them from behind or flush them out so those in the house can get a shot without hitting us. You ready?"

"As ready as I'm gonna get. Let's git'r done. I'm getting hungry."

Both men replaced partial magazines in their rifles with a full one, dropping the partials in their left side dump pouch. Andy counted down and then the two were running toward the fence, angling to get an angle behind the attackers, firing aimed shots as they ran forward. Two of the five men died where they lay, but the other three turned around and began to fire at Andy and Melvin.

Melvin went down with a cry, but Fargo and Nathan were adding their fire to that coming from the house. Two of the last three went down in the cross fire, but the third, with the best protection, was still firing.

Andy was at the fence and dropped to prone, mostly because he intended to, and partly because a bullet hit him in his left thigh, forcing him down. He fired several times, but between hitting the heavy chain link fence and his aim being disrupted by it, missed. Andy changed magazines and tried again.

The man was desperate. He rose and began to run toward the back of the property. He didn't make three steps before he went down.

Andy managed to get the MURS radio up to his lips. "Melvin and I are down. Anyone else hurt?"

"We're on our way!" Cathy shouted into her headset. The mike was still keyed when she told Karen to hang on.

Andy rolled onto his back, breathing heavily, trying to control the pain in his leg with concentration. It helped, but the leg still hurt. He turned his head and saw the two ATVs speeding toward him. He admired the driving skills of Cathy and Julie for a moment, but then passed out.

It was an hour later when he woke up, feeling queasy and needing to go to the bathroom. He opened his eyes and saw his entire extended family grouped around him. "How's Melvin? Anyone else hurt?"

"I'm fine," Melvin said. "Bullet bounced off my thick skull." Melvin was leaning rather heavily against Julie, but he was smiling.

"You're the only one with a serious injury," Jo-An said.

Cathy sat down on the edge of the bed and took one of Andy's hands in hers. "Everyone here on the farm is fine. Couple of minor things, but no serious gunshot wounds."

"Good. How is the prisoner?"

"He's fine," Jo-An said. "I checked him over. Not a scratch on him." Jo-An looked at Fargo.

"We persuaded him to leave and not come back," Fargo said. "If he survives, and I doubt he will, he won't ever come back this way."

Andy nodded and then asked, "Who got Alfred? I never did see him."

All other eyes turned to Casper, who was suddenly looking down at the floor.

"You should have seen him, Daddy! Casper saved all of us at the trees!" Jess was so excited she couldn't continue.

Andy looked at Jo-An. "She's right," Jo-An said. "We got the all clear and were coming in on the road when that monster truck of Alfred's came barreling down on us. He was going to run right over us. I grabbed Jess and pushed Mathew, trying to get them out of the way. Leslie jumped into the side ditch and began to fire, but she didn't have a good angle on Alfred. She made a sieve out of the passenger side of the truck and the tires.

But Casper stood his ground and opened up on Alfred. I don't know how many rounds hit the windshield before it finally broke, but it did break and Casper's last few rounds took Alfred in the chest and face.

"He just managed to jump clear as Alfred slumped forward, his body turning the steering wheel enough to send the truck into a skid, and then a series of rolls. It wasn't very pretty."

"Good work, Casper!" Andy said. "You okay?"

"It was scary, Uncle Andy. But Dad said I did okay."

"More than 'okay'," Fargo said proudly. "You did me and everyone else proud."

"Can I keep the carbine?" Casper asked.

Everyone laughed. "It's yours until you don't need it anymore," Andy said. "Speaking of which…"

"It's bad, Andy," Fargo said as the family went quiet. Brandon has been monitoring everything since the first day. We've taken dozens of nukes all across the country. Apparently got off our own in retaliation. It's what Tired Old Man calls GTW. Global Thermonuclear War."

"How's the farm set?"

Nathan answered. "I went over everything with Brandon. Everything went just the way we planned, except for the attack. It came much sooner than expected and the defenses just weren't all on-line when the shooting started. But the farm is okay. We'll be in a position to help with reconstruction and recovery as soon as it can be started. Fallout began just a few minutes ago."

"We sure cut this little family emergency excursion close, didn't we?" Andy asked, leaning back against the pillows. "I… ah… need to go to the bathroom. Will you guys all excuse me?"

There were nods all around and the family members began to leave, headed off to do their part to keep the farm running and a viable source of food for the entire area, once the fallout faded to safe levels.

I'LL HAVE A BEER, THANKS FOR ASKING

By

JERRY D. YOUNG

CHAPTER ONE

–

Barney slid the empty beer bottle across the width of the bar. "Another one, Trudy," he said as he slipped another twenty-dollar bill into the video poker machine in the bar surface. It was some moments before he looked up. A cold beer wasn't within reach of his right hand. Barney frowned and looked first left, and then to the right. There was Trudy, standing there near the end of the bar, staring up at the television.

Several people were crowding around, also watching the TV. Barney hesitated to prompt Trudy about his beer. It didn't pay to tick Trudy off. He could wait another minute. Or so. His eyes lifted from Trudy's rear to the TV.

"Holy Mackerel!" Barney exclaimed at the sight of a nuclear mushroom cloud rising. Then he hunched down, hoping no one had heard him. "Just that new show, Jericho," he thought to himself. "It's about a nuclear war."

He was about to ask Trudy again for that beer, but he noticed one of the women had turned to the man with her and buried her face in his

1

shoulder. She was crying. Great big sobbing gasps crying.

It finally dawned on Barney that something was wrong. "What's wrong? What's going on?" He asked. No one answered. "Hey," he said then, touching on a shoulder one of the men watching the TV with so much interest. "What's going on?"

This time he got a response. "Nuclear war has started. That's New York on the screen, you big dummy." Normally a comment like that would have resulted in Barney taking a swing at the one that voiced it, but the news was so astonishing that Barney didn't think to hit the man. He just stared at the screen with the rest of the bar patrons.

It finally came to him that he ought to do something. It was nuclear war. Just the one so far, but... The screen went white, and then black, and then another shot of a rising mushroom cloud, seen from a distance. Even Barney could tell it was a different one.

Now several people were crying and there was some soft cursing, that Barney couldn't quite make out. Oh. Maybe that was a prayer. Suddenly galvanized into action, being this was the real thing, Barney hit the cash out button on the video poker machine.

"Come on, Trudy! Cash me out. I need to get out of here and do... something! Oh. Get me a six-pack to go out of that." He grabbed the six-pack and his change, choosing a bill at random to shove across the bar. Trudy stared at it in awe. It was a five-dollar bill. Barney had never tipped more than the coin change from his beers. She looked up to thank him, but the door was closing as Barney strode out of the bar, on a mission.

Problem was Barney didn't know what the mission was. He climbed into his junker of a truck, an old Ford F-250 two-wheel-drive he'd got from his uncle for doing some plumbing work for him one time. Barney put the six-pack in the twelve-volt cooler. The six-pack was now a five-pack, since he'd pulled one bottle free and opened it with the opener on his keychain.

Putting the beer between his legs, Barney started the truck and then put it in gear. Where to go? Where to go? Nuclear war meant fallout. That was for sure. And that was dangerous. Where to go? Where to go? Barney suddenly hit the steering wheel with the heel of his right hand. "That culvert under the interstate for the X Bar X cattle cross-over!" he exclaimed, pressing the accelerator of the truck to pull out onto the street from the bar gravel parking lot.

"Gonna need food. Gonna need food. And water." Barney looked at the cooler. "More beer. Lot's more beer." He headed for the grocery store on the other end of town. The nearest one was closed. He was past his bank before he thought about it. He came to a screeching halt in the middle of the street, checked the rearview mirror and backed up until he could turn in to the ATM lane of the bank. "Work! Work! Work! Work!" he mumbled as he screeched to another halt, approximately across from the ATM panel. Barney fished the tattered leather wallet from his left hip pocket, took out the card, and slid it into the machine. "Yes!" he almost yelled when the screen came up with his options.

He knew how much he had in the bank, to the penny. He kept close track of his money. He had to. After punching in the total amount on deposit to withdraw, he got the error screen reminding him to withdraw in multiples of twenty dollars. "Nuts!" He punched in the new amount, which left $9.88 in the account. That irked him, but he let it go.

This was all he had. The rent money for this month coming up and the next, and enough for utilities and food for the two months. But that was it. Since he'd been laid off at the mine the handyman jobs he'd been getting were barely paying his way.

"Next stop, Cleppers Grocery!" The tires of the truck chirped as he dropped it into gear and hit the accelerator. The truck might not look like much, but Barney kept the engine tuned to a T.

He tried to calm himself down and not give away what he was doing so no one would beat him to what he wanted. It didn't look like anyone in the store knew what was going on. Grabbing a cart Barney headed for the liquor isle. Four twenty-four packs went into it. He rolled it up to the ice machine and got several sacks of ice for the beer.

Barney left the beer cart near the checkout lanes and grabbed another cart. He went straight to the canned meat isle. He raked can after can of roast beef, chili, and tuna fish into the cart.

Barney was almost running when he moved on to the canned vegetable and fruit aisle. Ignoring the vegetables for the most part, except for whole peeled tomatoes and pork and beans, he added quite a few cans of peaches.

He slid to a halt when he passed the display of jerky. He took all they had. Ditto the dried fruit. Except prunes. He hated prunes. Barney threw in half a dozen loaves of bread, and a couple big boxes of crackers.

Barney used paper towels for napkins so he decided to get a couple of rolls. Then he saw the toilet paper. Last time he'd been camping he'd run out of toilet paper. Not again. He grabbed the cheapest big package on the shelf. The second cart was overflowing.

He grabbed a shelf stocker and asked him to get him ten cases of the cheapest cases of water they had. "Liters or bigger."

When he got to the checkout stand with the two carts he'd filled, the high-school girl at the cash register looked amazed as she began to ring up Barney's purchases. "You never buy this much. You come into some money?"

Barney had a sickly look on his face. "Yeah. Something like that." He noticed the candy as he tried to look nonchalant. He went to each checkout lane and gathered up all the boxes of plain Hershey bars they had. He added them to the pile of stuff already on the sliding belt.

"I've got water coming," Barney said, as the clerk rang up the last of the candy. He looked around and pointed. "There he is."

The girl leaned over slightly to see what was coming and began to ring it up. "Ten cases," Barney told her. She nodded and ran up the final bill. Barney blanched.

The boy left the water on the trolley and followed Barney out to the truck. It was full dark now. The stars were bright, with the moon not up yet. Barney piled the groceries on the front passenger seat and floorboard and the water in the bed of the truck. The beer and ice went into the two coolers also in the bed of the truck. Barney suddenly looked up and noticed the stars. And a couple of streaks of bright white light heading west.

And then the lights in the store went out. Barney started the truck and headed home to get his camping gear. It didn't amount to much. A good tarp, some tent pegs, and a couple of poles with lots of 550 cord. An old GI sleeping bag he'd picked up. A fire grate. A coffee can stove and a couple more coffee cans for cook ware. A Coleman lamp and a couple of cans of fuel. A couple of ammo cans with the small stuff. He threw everything in the back of the truck, on top of his tools. It took a couple of minutes to get the little fresh food he had in the fridge out and put into the chiller box on the front seat.

With a last look around the efficiency apartment, Barney grabbed one kitchen chair and decided there wasn't anything else he really needed. He went out to the truck, got in and headed to the interstate. He couldn't figure out why he was passing so many cars on the road. From what he could see, he was the only thing moving. A couple of people tried to wave him down, but he just drove around them and ignored the cursing and rude gestures.

Barney took the next exit, and got on the service road. It ran out and he was on a dirt ranch road. Two miles further and he was at the cattle crossing underpass. There had been a lot of rain early that spring and both ends of the tunnel had piles of earth washed up from the drainage of the interstate. That worked to his advantage.

He didn't know much about radiation, but Barney did know mass was good. Taking a shovel from the bed of the truck, he worked on the two piles to make them as high as possible and as close to the tunnel as he could get them without moving the whole pile.

Using the reflected light from the truck headlights, Barney moved the food, water and beer from the truck into the tunnel, and then his camp gear and the chair. He started to set up the tarp as a lean-to but realized that the sand that had washed into the tunnel wasn't deep enough to hold the pegs.

So, he stacked the food and water to hold the poles in place and as anchors for tying off the lean-to. He put down the sleeping bag on the floor flap of the lean-to, and then lit the Coleman lantern. Barney went back outside, got an axe from the bed of the truck and began to cut sage-brush. Every so often he would stop cutting and carry the smelly stuff into the tunnel. When he had a pile of firewood large enough to suit him, he put the axe back in the truck, turned off the headlights, and went back into the tunnel.

Five more beers on top of the ones he'd had at the bar and the one in the truck and Barney was ready for bed. He'd done all he knew to do. Time would tell if it was enough. Hopefully it would be a little war.

CHAPTER TWO

-

When Barney came groggily awake the next morning it took a few seconds for him to remember where he was. When he did, he scrambled up and started for the south end of the tunnel. He stopped before he got close. The sky wasn't very bright. He checked his watch. The sun was up. Then he noticed the dust falling. It was almost like a rain of very tiny dry raindrops. He backed up.

He stopped and thought for a few moments and then decided to do his business inside the tunnel. He picked a spot, scraped the sand away and did what he needed to do, and then covered things back up.

Rubbing the stubble on his chin, Barney realized he hadn't brought any shaving gear. With the thought in his mind about what else he might have forgotten to bring, he started to fix breakfast. He came to an abrupt stop, can of corned beef hash in his hand. He hadn't brought a can opener. The corned beef hash had a self-opener, but not everything did. He hated the thought of using his good sheath knife to open tin cans, but that was about his only option.

Then again, maybe not. The sheath knife was nowhere to be found in the ammo box that held the small items of camping gear. For the life of him he couldn't remember what he'd done with it. That meant it was the pocket knife. "Nuts!"

After a breakfast of the two eggs he'd brought from home, and the can of corned beef hash, Barney looked at the fallout coming down and wondered if he was going to live or die. Some-thing else he realized he hadn't thought of was something to do. There were several books at home he'd never got around to reading.

Barney dropped his head on his chest for a moment. "Guess I can sleep all I want to." Which was what he did mostly, during the two weeks he waited, after the fallout stopped. He seemed to remember that two weeks was somehow important. But the morning of the second day he couldn't keep anything on his stomach. He threw up, off and on, all day and decided he was going to die. But he'd go out fighting.

He felt much better the next day and was able to keep some food down. Maybe he wouldn't die, after all. Realizing that he didn't have any first-aid kit beyond a couple of Band-Aids and a twelve count tin of Excedrin, Barney became very cautious opening the tins of food with his pocket knife. It was sharp to start with, but dulled rapidly. He worked it on the concrete to keep it as sharp as he could. It was something to do, and a sharp knife is safer than a dull one.

As the two-week point rolled around, Barney noticed he was taking much more hair from his comb whenever he combed it, than usual. Didn't that mean he had radiation sickness? He was pretty sure it did. But he sure didn't feel like he was about to die. For the most part, other than feeling kind of tired, despite all the sleep, he didn't feel all that bad. But the beer was long gone, though he still had plenty of food. Water was running low, but he still had enough. He was just ready to leave the tunnel.

He waffled back and forth for an hour about whether or not to pack up everything he had left and take it with him, or leave it in the tunnel. He hadn't seen or heard a soul since he'd been there, but he figured with his luck, someone would wander in and steal everything if he left it. But then again, the same thing might happen if he took it with him. Someone might try to take what he had.

Barney compromised. After digging into the mound of earth at each end of the tunnel, he split his supplies and buried two-thirds of what was left, a third in each hole. The other third he would take with him.

So Barney headed back to town. When he left the interstate and got back on the local road into town he still hadn't seen anyone. Just all those cars stopped on the highway. Actually he couldn't quite say that. He'd seen two dead bodies in one of them. He didn't realize it until he happily pulled over and got out of the truck to talk to them. He felt like throwing up again.

He did see a couple of people running away from Cleppers. The windows were all busted out and carts and parts of shelving units lay scattered around the parking lot. Barney pulled into the parking lot and went into the store. It was stripped of everything edible or immediately useable. Just hardware and non-edible things were left. Barney shook his head. "Looters," he said, going back to the truck. It surprised him when he saw the two that had run away edging back toward the store. "Wait a minute! They're not going back to the store! They're headed for my truck!"

He ran the last few steps to the truck. "Hey! You guys! What do you want? Do you know what happened? Where is everyone?"

Neither of the two men, looking to be in their mid- to late-twenties, replied. One brought up a baseball bat from where he had been holding it against his right leg. The other unsheathed a wicked looking knife.

Fire in his eye, Barney reached into the bed of the truck and brought out the axe. If they wanted a fight, they'd get it. When the two saw the axe they exchanged a quick look, then turned and ran off again. One didn't get very far. He came to a sliding halt and began to throw up.

Barney got into the truck and drove off, wishing he hadn't sold his old Winchester .30-30 for beer money three years before. It looked like every window on main street was busted and the buildings looted. Deciding that the most probable place to find someone would be at city hall, or the county offices. He tried the city hall, but no one was around. It looked intact.

His next stop, at the county office complex, was more interesting. Barney saw activity through a couple of windows, so parked the truck and headed for the front door. He looked all around before he started to go inside. He didn't get a chance to open the door. It seemed to open on its own and he was staring into the business end of an AR-15.

Barney's hands went up and he took a step back. "Hold it right there!" came a firm voice.

"What's going on? I haven't done anything!"

"Are you one of them?"

"Them who?"

"The raiders. They came through two days ago. Some of us holed up here. We haven't been out since."

"No. I've been hiding out outside of town. I just came in to see what was going on," Barney started to lower his hands but the muzzle of the AR-15 made two upward jerks and his hands went back up.

"Well, who all is in there? Maybe someone knows me. I'm Barney Richardson."

From well back in the building came a whiney voice. "It's Barney Fife. Yeah. I know him. We're drinking buddies."

Barney didn't challenge the statement since the AR-15 was lowering. Him and Jim Perkins were not drinking buddies. The little slug was always calling him Barney Fife. Barney hated that.

"Look," Barney lowered his hands. "I haven't seen any raiders, or signs of them. Well, except for all the businesses look like they've been looted."

"You have any food?" came a call from those behind. Barney wasn't surprised it was the same voice as before. "We haven't had anything to eat since day before yesterday."

"Well..." Barney hesitated. Not saying yes didn't do any good. Three people pushed past the guy holding the AR-15 and headed for Barney's truck, including Jim. "Hey!" Barney called out as they started going through it. He started to step down toward them to stop the scavenging, but the AR-15 was pointing at him again. Barney just frowned and let it go.

"Is there anyone in charge here?" Barney asked the gun holder, finally looking past the muzzle at the wielder. His eyes widened. It was a woman.

"I guess I am," she said. The AR-15 was finally hanging by her side, not pointing at him.

"I should know you. You look familiar." Barney was looking at her quizzically.

I'm Genevieve Prescott. Tom's daughter. The pharmacist. I used to handle the cash register some at his shop."

"Yeah. That's it. Where's Tom?"

A forlorn looked crossed Genevieve's face. "They killed him. The raiders. For the drugs." She shook her head. "And the drugs won't even help them. They'd been out in the radiation too much. Most of them were already in bad shape, but they were able to kill people and take what little food was left after the food riot."

"Food riot?"

"Yes. I'm ashamed to admit it, but the local residents mobbed both grocery stores and both mini-marts when it became obvious what was happening. I guess people don't keep much food at home anymore. It seemed like everyone was there."

Barney didn't mention his early visit to the store on that day. "So the raiders didn't do that, huh?"

She shook her head. "Most of the rest. Liquor stores and the pharmacy. A lot of the stores they just trashed for the pleasure, I guess."

Barney was keeping an eye on the truck. Food for hungry people… Okay. But Jim was starting to take out the 12-volt chiller from the cab. "Hey! Just the food!" Jim looked reluctant, but he put the chiller back down on the seat and got back out of the truck.

"How many people are here?" Barney asked.

"Twenty-three," Genevieve replied. "A couple of people left right after the raiders quit attacking us here, but we heard some shooting right after that. I don't know if it was them or someone else."

It was only then that Barney noticed the pockmarks on the stone building, mostly around windows. "How many were there?"

"Fifteen… Twenty… I'm not sure. But every one of them had at least two or three guns. It was all I could do to hold them off. And I'm about out of ammunition."

"You held them off by yourself?" Barney asked, incredulous. When she nodded he believed her.

"They took their dead and wounded, which surprised me, and left after shooting the place up. They only stayed across the street. Never tried to flank me, or attack the rear of the building. I'd never have been able to stop them if they had."

Barney still thought she had done a pretty good job, though he didn't say so. "You have any idea if the radiation is gone? Where did you shelter?"

"Over at City Hall. That building has a better basement than this one. Some of us just came out three days ago to check on things. The raiders caught us out. Never did get over to the hospital to check there. Some people were planning to shelter at it. Don't know about the radiation. I'm hoping they have some instruments over there. Fallout was physically light, but it might still have been pretty hot."

"Hot? Oh. Nuke hot."

Genevieve nodded. "We only saw a couple of vehicles running that day we were out and about. Yours seems to be doing okay. I guess it's old enough the EMP didn't damage it."

"EMP?" Barney asked.

"Yeah. Electro Magnetic Pulse. Don't you know what that is?"

Barney shook his head.

"Well, I don't have time to explain it to you. Uh… Is there any chance you can run me over to the hospital? I'm still leery about going out on my own. No one here has wanted to go. I guess they might, now."

"No, that's okay. I'll take you. Come on, let's go."

17

Genevieve reached down and picked up a large gym bag. At Barney's questioning look, she said, "Rest of my loaded magazines, plus the empties. Don't want to lose any." Barney nodded.

She turned around and gave some instructions to two people that had been hovering just out of earshot. "Find something to hold them and then go pick up all the empty brass you can find across the street. I'll be back for it. I'll try to find more food."

"Some of these people are like animals," Genevieve said softly as more people came out and started fighting with the first three over the food.

"Yeah. A couple of guys tried to steal my truck when I stopped at Cleppers to see what I could find."

"You've got a valuable property here, in a running vehicle, especially a truck." She looked over at him after she buckled her seatbelt. "You don't have to tell me and I'll understand, but do you have much gasoline?"

Barney almost didn't tell her, but he was beginning to trust her. "I'm something of a fanatic about fuel. Ran out once up in the mountains. I'd just filled the tanks the day before this happened. A twenty gallon and a forty-gallon tank under the truck and two 5-gallon cans in the back."

"Sweet. I'd hide as much of it as I could. They may start commandeering stuff like that. Maybe even the truck."

"They, who? Haven't seen any National Guard or anything. Have you?"

"No. But one of the guys that got caught out with us is a ham. He was picking up some traffic on one of the military bands before his batteries went dead. He said they had to be getting close. That was the day we came out of the basement. We were supposed to just try to get some more food and water since we were running short, but the raiders were there and chased us to the county offices."

"I stopped at the City Hall. I didn't see any signs of anyone."

"I told the ones that stayed behind to lay low unless I came back and gave a password to let them know everything was okay. I want to get to the hospital and see how it's going there before I go back to City Hall. I hate to go back without taking some food and water."

Barney turned down one street and had to back out. There were two cars dead on the street going opposite ways, side by side. He took the streets around them and finally got to the hospital without any additional trouble.

The stink was unmistakable when they opened the main door into the hospital. Genevieve and Barney both backed out of the lobby and began to retch, one on each side of the walkway. After a few minutes they made their way around the building, trying different doors. The smell was overwhelming at every one, until they got to the kitchen delivery door. It, too, was unlocked and Genevieve opened it a crack and took a cautious sniff. Discernable, but tolerable.

They went inside and tried the door from the kitchen to the dining area of the hospital. The smell was not quite as bad, but still sickening. Genevieve closed the door and turned back to the kitchen. "Let's see what we can find."

When they began opening cabinets they did find some #10 cans of food. It would be enough to feed everyone they knew about at least one meal. Maybe two for the children. Barney brought the truck around and they loaded everything edible into the bed of the truck, and then headed for City Hall. Barney made sure there was a can opener included.

When they got there, Genevieve ran to one of the basement access doors and banged on it. She gave the password and the door opened. When Barney got close he got a whiff of the air in the basement. It was nowhere near as sickening as the hospital, but it was rank enough. Too many people in too small a place with inadequate facilities.

Barney stayed outside, going back to the truck, while Genevieve went inside to come up with a plan with the others to feed everyone. When Genevieve came back out she told Barney they had decided to take everything to one of the restaurants near the edge of town that used propane for cooking. It should have what they needed, even if the place had been vandalized.

Everyone was to walk to it, while Barney took Genevieve and four other people to get things set up. The main window was broken and there were a few overturned chairs, but the place was intact. Barney went to check the propane tank. It was about half full. He checked the valve. It had been turned off. Someone had been thinking. He hoped it was one of the survivors.

Barney turned the valve on and then went back inside to light the pilot lights of the cook stoves. After that, with the others preparing the food, Barney felt a little redundant and went outside to his truck. Genevieve saw him leaving and followed him out. "You aren't leaving, are you?" she asked.

"I've done all I can, as far as I can see. I want to check on my apartment and make sure everything is okay." He rubbed his rather scraggly beard. "And I want to shave."

Genevieve smiled at him. "I can understand that." The smile faded. "But... We need more water."

"Gee. I don't know," Barney replied. He looked thoughtful. "We can check places here in town, but I bet there isn't a lot. I guess I could go check the city's tank. See if it still has water in it." The more he thought, the more ideas he had.

21

"I'll stop at the hardware store and get some plastic buckets. They sell them I think."

"Thanks, Barney," Genevieve said. "I'd go help, but I don't want to leave this group unprotected."

"Sure. No problem." Barney climbed into the truck and headed for the hardware store. It looked like the hardware store had been hit, too, but not badly. There weren't any firearms or ammunition left. Barney checked that first. But he found an even dozen 6-gallon plastic buckets with lids and loaded them into the truck. He also found a sheath knife that had been overlooked. He took that, too.

When he got to the water tank he felt elated when he saw the automatic generator sitting beside the pump house. But then he was disappointed when he checked it. Apparently it had worked like a charm when the power went out. It had run the fuel tank dry. The water tank was also dry. Barney cussed for a little while, and then got back into the truck

He drove down to the river and filled the buckets and his two coolers with river water. Barney had to stop often. He didn't think he'd ever been this tired, and he really hadn't done all that much. "Just the two weeks of doing nothing, I guess," he told the world after he loaded the tenth bucket of water into the bed of the truck. He left the other two empty. Barney stopped be-hind the hardware store after he left the river.

The hardware store rented tow-behind concrete mixers and had the cement and aggregates to make concrete. He half-filled one of the empty buckets with fine sand after removing the top layer that he figured had fallout on it. He got back into the truck and headed for Cleppers. There he found several packages of coffee filters.

Taking all they had, he put them on the front seat and went back to the diner. Genevieve came out when she saw the truck pull up. "Any luck?" she asked. She had the AR-15 slung over one shoulder and held a plate of food in one hand. She set the food on one of the outdoor tables and went over to the truck. "I'll help you."

"Well," said Barney, "It's a good news, bad news deal. The city tank was empty and so was the fuel tank for the generator. We might get that going if we can get fuel from the depot outside of town. For now, I got river water and the stuff to make a simple filter."

Genevieve watched as Barney poked several holes in the bottom of one of the buckets, near the center, and then placed several coffee filters on the inside bottom of the bucket. After transferring the sand from its bucket to the filter bucket, he set the empty bucket on the ground near the entrance of the diner. Barney cut a large circle out of the middle of the lid for the empty bucket, snapped it into place, and set the filter bucket on top of the empty bucket.

"Can you get me something to dip the water with?" he asked Genevieve.

She took her food with her back inside and came out a few moments later with a large pot. Barney had just finished putting a layer of coffee filters on top of the sand in the filter bucket. Bringing one of the water buckets over, he took off the lid and began to ladle water into the filter bucket.

"Going to take a while, but just keep adding water to the top bucket and taking it out of the bottom one. This will filter stuff out, but it won't help if there is some kind of bug or something in the water. It's all I know to do."

"We'll just have to take a chance. Some of these people are desperate for water. Thanks, Barney."

Barney felt himself blush at her words. He hadn't blushed in years. "Sure," he replied, shrugging his shoulders. "No big deal. But I'm tired now. I'm going over to my apartment and get shaved and take a nap."

"Okay. Oh. Don't you want some food?"

Barney shook his head. "Too tired to eat. I'd probably just throw it up, anyway."

"Radiation sickness," Genevieve said, looking somber. "What kind of shelter were you in?"

After his explanation, Genevieve said, "Clever. But you probably got an unhealthy dose. I hope you'll be okay."

"Yeah. Me, too." With that, Barney got into the truck and went to his apartment. He started to go inside, but turned back and opened the hood of the Ford. Getting a screwdriver from the toolbox in the bed of the truck, Barney unsnapped the catches for the distributor cap and took out the rotor. No one was going to steal his truck without a lot of trouble.

Even with those precautions, after he carried one of the coolers of water inside and shaved, he came back outside and lay down across the seat in the truck to nap. Just in case.

It was well into the afternoon when Barney awakened. He rubbed his face with both hands and sat up. And found himself staring into the barrel of another firearm. A pump shotgun this time. "That truck wasn't here before. That means it runs. Get out. I'm taking it."

Barney lifted his eyes from the muzzle of the shotgun to the face of the man holding it. When his eyes uncrossed he noted that the man's hair had fallen out in patches. He was nearly bald. There were huge dark half-moons under his eyes. He did not look well at all. But he was holding the gun steady.

Easing out of the truck, Barney waited for his chance. He knew it would come. He'd been in a few fights in his time and knew how to take advantage of the other guy's mistakes. With the door half open, the muzzle of the shotgun still partly through the open window, Barney shoved the door the rest of the way open.

The door post hit the shotgun and swung it away from Barney. The man fired in reflex, the shot charge going over the hood of the truck. Barney tackled the man, taking both of them to the ground. Landing on the man cushioned Barney's fall and knocked the wind out of the man. Barney slugged him a couple of times, knocking the man out with the second punch.

Barney climbed to his feet, the shotgun in his hands. He frisked the man and recovered half a dozen 12 gauge shells. All 7½ shot. He checked the magazine. It still held three rounds. He reloaded the shotgun and set it in the truck.

Then he bent down to try to bring the guy around with a slap or two, if need be. But when Barney knelt down and shook the man, his head rolled back and forth rather uncannily. Alarmed, Barney checked the man's pulse in his throat. He couldn't find one. Barney watched the man's chest for a couple of minutes. It neither rose nor fell. The man was dead.

Barney blanched, rose, and stepped back. He'd never killed anyone before. It was a feeling he didn't like. Even if it was more or less accidental. Barney finally shrugged. "Probably would have died, anyway, the way he looks."

Barney wondered what to do with the body for a few minutes. When he came to a decision he loaded the body in the back of the truck. It was a struggle that left him gasping for breath. He rested for a few moments and then installed the rotor in the distributor. He got in the truck, started it and headed for one of the cemeteries outside of town. That's where dead bodies belonged, he had decided.

After pulling the body out of the truck, Barney dragged it over to an empty plot and left it there. Feeling more than a little sick, Barney went back to his tunnel shelter to spend the rest of the afternoon taking a nap. Nothing had been disturbed in his absence. He woke up as it was get-ting dark. Barney opened a can of roast beef for supper. It was easier now. It was easier with the can opener he'd filched at the hospital kitchen when he got the one to take to the diner. After his supper he went back to bed and was asleep again in moments. It had been a stressful and tiring day.

CHAPTER THREE

-

The next morning, during his breakfast, Barney debated on whether or not to go back into town or wait a few more days. The cooler and a half of water would let him save the rest of his bottled water. He had a couple of bottles of Potable Aqua in his camp gear.

His conscience finally got the best of him, after he'd decided to stay where he was for another week or so and let the townspeople work things out on their own. His was the only working vehicle so far. They might need him to help with something.

This time Barney loaded up his gear, leaving the one cache were it was, but taking every-thing out of the first one. He wasn't in any big hurry, so he stopped at several of the cars abandoned on the highway and siphoned what gas he could get. He kept a siphon hose in the truck to transfer fuel from the 5-gallon cans. He always spilled too much when he tried to pour it in. Barney managed to top up both truck tanks and refill both the cans.

He slammed on his brakes just after he'd passed a semi that had managed to get onto the shoulder before it quit rolling after it died. It was a grocery delivery truck. "Be full. Be full. Be full. Be full," he chanted as he walked to the rear of the trailer. No lock. Not a good sign. Barney opened the rear doors anyway. And found a treasure trove. It wasn't full, but it was three-quarters full.

Barney climbed inside and began to check the pallets. It was mostly food, but there were some dry goods as well. He loaded up the back of the Ford with general selections and then closed the doors to the trailer. He took a lock out of his toolbox and locked the trailer doors.

When he got to town, he drove by the diner. No one was there. He went to City hall. There were people lounging around and he saw Genevieve keeping watch from the tall steps up to the main entrance. He waved her over. He began to untie and roll back the tarp with which he'd covered the contents of the bed of the truck.

"Holy cow, Barney! Where'd you get all this?"

"Found it. Okay? Don't ask too many questions."

Genevieve grinned at him. "Whatever you say." She called several of the people over to help unload. Most of the food could be eaten from the can or package.

"We've got people out scavenging for food, but they aren't having much luck. People don't keep a lot of food at home any more, I guess," she said as the food was unloaded. Barney had noticed the wheel-barrows and garden carts sitting on the lawn.

"You're all still sleeping in the basement of the City Hall?" Barney asked as more people streamed out to help.

Genevieve nodded. "We still don't know what the radiation level is. We've kept an AM/FM radio watch going, but there hasn't been any local news. We occasionally get a station from way off, so we know there are more survivors, but haven't heard anything even remotely local.

"Some of the people have pretty bad radiation sickness," she continued, "From what I know about it, several of them are going to die. And we're keeping the kids inside, except for just a few minutes a day. They have the highest risk."

"I think I've got it," Barney admitted. "I was sick for a couple of days and my hair is coming out. And I'm so weak all the time. It was all I could do yesterday. And today, loading up the food wore me completely out."

"Those are all signs, for sure. But it sounds like a moderate dose. Maybe it won't be too bad."

"I hope not." Suddenly Barney straightened up, from his leaning position against the truck. "Something just occurred to me. I gotta go."

"What?" Genevieve asked, but Barney just waved and drove off.

Barney drove all the way across town and out into the country. He'd remembered talking to a drunk at a street fair several years ago. The guy had been bragging how prepared he was for the end of the world. It was only later that Barney found out the guy's name. He'd driven by his place not long after that. It looked ordinary and Barney forgot all about it, until now.

When Barney got to the place his smile faded. Apparently the guy had bragged a little too much a little too often. Or the man had just been unlucky. The house was half burned down. When Barney got out and cautiously approached he saw the remains of a human form lying in the carnage, a rifle still in one hand. The garage was still intact. Barney checked it. If there had been anything in it, it was gone.

Barney tried to remember more about the conversation. He'd been a bit drunk himself and the memory was sketchy. But something was nagging at Barney. Something in the conversation about split supplies so if the government started confiscating things, they'd find some and quit looking. Barney was sure the man hadn't mentioned the actual location, but there had been two or three clues the guy let slip.

One was that it was on his property but what where the rest?

Walking around the place, Barney hoped he would see something that would jog his memory. He saw a small out building in the back yard and went to investigate it. It was the pump house. There had been something about the pump house. He couldn't see anything inside, except the water line coming out of the well into a tank, and the power line going into the well.

And the electrical box. Barney remembered something the guy had said. "They'd never think to look in a breaker." Barney hadn't any idea at the time, but now it might make sense. He opened the electrical panel and used his knife to undo the screws holding the internal cover in place. One of the breakers was marked 'Spare' on the listing on the door. There were no wires leading from it. He pulled it free of the electrical bus and shook it. Sure enough, it rattled.

Using the tip of his pocket knife this time, Barney undid the screws holding the breaker together and found a key. Okay. Now he had a key. Where was the lock that it fit? Something about birdbrains never finding it. The word birdbrains seemed hysterically funny to the guy.

Barney had walked past an overturned bird bath on the way to the pump house. Hurrying now, Barney went to the truck and got a shovel. It was the work of only a few minutes to dig down where the bird bath had stood. Something thudded and Barney made the hole a bit bigger, exposing a square panel made of treated boards. And there was a lock, wrapped in duct tape.

After removing the tape from the lock, Barney tried the key. Sure enough, it worked. He opened the hatch and looked down into darkness. Back to the truck to get a flashlight. There was a ladder down into the hole and Barney took it. He had to crouch down, the concrete compartment had a low ceiling.

Barney decided it was a two-thousand-gallon septic tank. And it was nearly filled with boxes and other containers, all neatly labeled. They were stacked along the two sides of the tank, floor to ceiling, two deep, with a very narrow center aisle between.

A wooden cabinet was at the far end of the aisle. It had a lock on it as well. Barney tried the key. It worked. Swinging the door open, Barney decided he didn't have to worry about only having the pump shotgun and a few shells for it. The cabinet was a small armory. The long guns were racked; the handguns were on a shelf. Barney saw the ammunition cans stacked two deep by two wide by four high on both sides of the cabinet.

The man must have built the cabinet in place, because it was too big to have come through the hatch, Barney decided. Some of the boxes, it looked like to him, would barely fit through the hatch. Checking the labels of the boxes next to the aisle, and then pulling three to check the la-bels on the boxes against the wall, Barney determined that the box behind held the same or similar items as the box on the aisle. Might not be true for all, but for Barney's mental inventory, he assumed so. He whistled. This was a lot of stuff.

Leaning over was hurting his back, so he turned back to the entrance. That's when he saw the clipboard laying on top of the left hand row of boxes. It was a detailed inventory. And it answered a question that had popped into his mind. The man had stored all of this. Wouldn't he have stored fuel, too?

He had. It was in 55-gallon drums, which were, in turn, placed in over-pack barrels buried around the perimeter of the tank.

Barney didn't get greedy. He took a Springfield Armory 1911 .45 ACP, six spare magazines, which were in one of the boxes stacked next to the cabinet, and a Ruger Ranch Rifle, also with six spare magazines.

Opening one of the ammo cans marked .223/5.56, Barney took out three bandoleers. One would fill the magazines and the other two were spare reloads. Out of one of the .45 ACP cans came two boxes of ball ammunition. Barney also took two boxes of 12-gauge shotgun shells. 00-Buck. One of the weapons related boxes contain a couple of cleaning kits. He took one of those, too.

He almost forgot what had sent him on this chase in the first place. He found the container that held electrical equipment. He took out a CD V-715 radiation survey meter and a couple of batteries.

After setting the weapons and accessories outside, Barney climbed out, closed and locked the door hatch and carefully refilled the hole, placing the sod he'd cut out back on top. He stood the bird bath back up on top of the hole.

He put a battery in the meter and tried it. Best he could figure out the reading was 0.30 R-something.

He was hungry and his back hurt when he got back to his apartment. He took the same precaution he had before, pulling the rotor out of the distributor before he went upstairs to his apartment. It took him three trips to get the things he wanted from the truck.

Barney ate a little and then set about field stripping the weapons and cleaning them. He loaded up the magazines and wished he had something to carry them in besides his pockets. There was load bearing gear in the tank, but it was in one of the back, bottom boxes and he hadn't wanted to dig that deep yet. Besides, he wanted something a little less obvious and military looking.

After he rested for a while, Barney went back down to City Hall. Again Genevieve was on watch. He waved her over. "Has anyone run across a generator?" he asked.

"No. We're looking, but haven't run across one."

"I'm going to go out and check Fernando's place. He had a portable generator for running tools and stuff. I worked for him some. It'll make it a lot easier to get water we don't have to filter."

"Thank you, Barney. That's sweet of you. And by the way, Jasper said he thought he could get a couple of vehicles going if he gets the parts from the auto supply store. He doesn't want to go on his own and people are getting sick right and left now. Everyone else is out scavenging. We're getting a few things, but what you brought sure kept us going."

"I'll take him with me. And don't worry. I'll bring another load of food in tomorrow. Oh. And I found this." He handed her the CD V-715.

She didn't ask him where he got it. "Thanks again, Barney. I'll go send Jasper out." She hadn't mentioned anything about the weapons now on the seat of the truck, either.

It wasn't far to the auto parts store. Jasper said it would take a while to find everything he needed. Barney nodded. "I'll hang around out here."

As he was waited, thinking about trying to find some beer, he noticed the women's clothing store across the street. On a hunch, he went over and stepped through the broken window. He found the purse section and found what he thought he might. It was a large shoulder bag, of leather. He whistled when he saw the price. It just about cleaned him out, but he left money at the cash register. He didn't feel right about taking something like this without paying for it. Food and water were one thing. And if the owner of something was obviously not coming back, he figured it was okay.

Back at the truck, he put the magazines for the pistol and rifle in different compartments of the bag and put the strap over his head, onto his shoulder. He took it back off to adjust the shoulder strap length. It worked well when he put it back on. He had his LBE.

Barney was a pretty good shade tree mechanic, but he didn't have much experience with newer models. He acted as a second pair of hands for Jasper as he worked on three different vehicles. Two started and ran all right. The third would start, but only run for a few seconds before dying.

"I don't know," Jasper said, "There must be another computer or something that I don't know about." He pulled the parts he'd put in, and then they shuttled the other two vehicles back to City Hall. One was a Jeep Cherokee, and the other a Ford pickup, both mid-eighties models.

Again Barney was exhausted well before nightfall. Afraid of something happening to the truck, even if he pulled the rotor, he went back to his tunnel. He just laid the tarp out, put his sleeping bag down, climbed in, and pulled the tarp over him.

He was still feeling poorly the next morning when he had his breakfast. But he'd told Genevieve he would deliver another load of food. And he hadn't made it out to Fernando's the day before. With a sigh, Barney got into the truck and went to work.

By the time he had to quit early that afternoon, he had a small generator hooked up to a private well with a pump there in town. The city residents could get safe water fairly easily now. They just had to bring their own container.

When he went back to City Hall to tell Genevieve, she scolded him for doing too much. Apparently he didn't look too well.

"The radiation is still way over 0.10. Almost 0.30. Everyone is still getting pretty bad doses of radiation when they are out doing stuff. I didn't know. I wouldn't have let anyone leave the shelter if I'd known how high it was."

"We all going to die?" Barney asked Genevieve.

"Oh, no. Some will, but even at these doses, most people will only show some of the symptoms. What worries me is the flu or something getting started. Everyone's immune system is very weak. The flu could kill a bunch. I suggest you stay here in the shelter for a few days. It has to be better than your tunnel."

"Well, thanks." Barney wasn't inclined to stay in town. Apparently his tunnel had protected him well enough to get through the worst of it. It would do for the rest of it. "When do we not have to worry about the radiation? Do you know?"

"When it's down below 0.10. It will still be affecting people, but at that level its mostly long term effects, if you don't already have a big accumulated dose. I'm not sure how long that will be. I know the seven ten rule, but I don't have enough numbers to figure out the rates previous to when you gave me the meter. We just have to keep measuring it every day until the meter says 0.10."

"Okay," Barney replied. "I'm going back out to my tunnel. I probably won't come in for two or three days. The food good for that long?"

"I think so. Thanks again for all that. The curiosity is killing me about where you're getting it, but I said I wouldn't ask too many questions."

Barney managed a smile. "Thanks." With a wave of his hand out the open window of the truck, Barney drove off. He was feeling much better three days later when he headed back into town. He became concerned when he thought he heard weapons fire. He stopped the truck and listened. Yes. There was definitely a fire fight going on in town.

Keeping a sharp eye out, Barney drove as close to the noise as he dared. He pulled the rotor again, and slipped the .45 behind his belt in the small of his back. Slinging the musette bag with the magazines over his head and onto his right shoulder, Barney picked up the Ranch Rifle. Taking his time, he approached the area of the fire fight. It was at the City Hall.

He spotted one of the attackers. It was a man in uniform. Barney was hesitant to fire on the military. Maybe it was just a misunderstanding he could clear up. He changed his mind when another man, also in uniform, bellowed out what he was going to do to the women when he got to them.

Barney used all his deer hunting scouting skills to locate most of the attack force. They were all in uniform. He found a National Guard Humvee parked out of harm's way. A soldier with a lieutenant's bar lay dead nearby.

Barney made his way back to the fight, a plan in mind. He'd use the Sgt. York turkey hunting tactic of taking out the rearmost soldier and advancing to the next. That would give him the best chance of taking out a few of them before they discovered him.

Sighting carefully, Barney squeezed the trigger of his rifle. He had fired a couple of sighting shots out at the tunnel, so he knew the sights were on. The man fell silently. Barney advanced. He took out three more of the soldiers before he drew the attention of the rest.

He started taking fire, but the attack from the rear had spooked the rest. With Genevieve and someone else firing from City Hall, and the attack from their rear, the last four began to withdraw headed Barney was sure, for the Humvee. He broke into a run to cut them off.

Barney almost ran right into one of the men. He fired from the hip and the man fell. Barney slowed then and eased closer to the Humvee. The shot he'd taken nearby slowed the others' advance.

After seeing one man ease his head around the corner of a building to check the Humvee, Barney waited until he moved again. The shot took him clean. The other two men made a mad dash for the vehicle. Barney poured fire at them, but had to reload. His next shot took one of the men down, but the other got into the Humvee. Barney ran forward and shot him at close range before he could get the vehicle started.

Everything fell silent. Barney checked each of his targets in turn. All but the one he'd almost run into was dead. He left that one where he lay. He wasn't going anywhere. Not one-hundred-percent sure that was everyone, Barney headed toward the City Hall. He also didn't want to get shot by someone there, either.

He didn't find anyone else, just a few more dead bodies. He called out to the City Hall from cover, just in case. It was Genevieve that returned his call. He spun around suddenly when he heard the Humvee start and take off with a squeal of tires. There had been someone else.

People began to come out of the building, making Barney uneasy. There could be more around. But nothing happened and people spread out and began collecting weapons and such from the dead soldiers. Other's lay lamenting over the fallen bodies of their own killed.

"They took us by surprise," Genevieve told Barney when she joined him. "From some of the coherent yelling I take it they had sneaked into town and scouted out likely targets. Most of us were outside when the first volley came from over here. That's what got most of our people dead. I did what I could. So did Jimmy. He'd found a bolt action and some ammunition in one of the houses he searched. I know we got two or three of them, but you turned the battle. How did you know we were in trouble?"

"I didn't. I just happened to be coming into town and heard the firing." Barney and Genevieve both spun around, their weapons rising, as a shot rang out."

"Be careful," Barney yelled. "There's a live injured one out there."

"Not anymore," came the cheerful, yelled reply.

"I believe the spoils go to the victor," Genevieve said, as several people came up showing them what they were finding. You get

42

your pick. What you don't want goes into the communal supplies.

Barney started to decline, considering what he had in his new stash, but decided more is usually better. He took a couple of the M-4's, three dozen magazines, and a couple of nice non-issue knives. There was only one pistol among the salvaged items and it was an M-9 9mm. He left it for the community. Apparently any extra ammunition was in the Humvee. None of the soldiers had been carrying bandoleers, just their loaded magazines. Barney was amazed they had been firing full-auto with only the few magazines each soldier had.

He went to his truck and put the weapons away, and then drove back to the City Hall, joining Genevieve again in front of the building, still carrying the Ranch Rifle.

"Hey!" a youth yelled, running up to them. "Look what I found! It's an Army walky-talky!"

He handed it to Genevieve. She keyed the radio and said, "This is Genevieve Prescott. Can anyone hear me?"

Almost immediately a voice came out of the speaker. "I hear you. Why are you on a military radio?" By the time Genevieve had explained a Blackhawk helicopter was hovering over them. It banked away and began landing in a nearby vacant lot.

A group of soldiers came running over, rifles at port arms, led by a Captain and a Lieutenant.

"We'll take charge of those," the Lieutenant said, going with his men to collect the 'spoils'. There was a medic in the squad and he began checking the fallen soldiers. When he returned, he went over to the Lieutenant and whispered in his ear.

The Captain had watched the gathering of the weaponry, silently, but then turned toward Genevieve and Barney. Everyone else had shied away, grouping together at the top of the stairs to the entrance of City Hall.

"Looks like you did the world a service and saved the National Guard some time and trouble. We've been after these guys for almost a week."

"At least one of them got away," Barney said. "In a Humvee."

"We saw it on the way here. It was stopped on the interstate, the driver lying on the road beside it. No sign of anyone else."

"One of us must have hit him," Genevieve said.

The Lieutenant came up to the Captain and asked, "Should we disarm the civilians, Sir?"

Both Genevieve and Barney stepped back and gripped their weapons tightly.

"I don't think that will be necessary, Lieutenant," said the Captain. "Carry on with gathering the bodies and all their belongings."

"Yes, sir," the Lieutenant replied, saluting, and then walking away. Barney didn't mention the stuff in the truck and if they didn't look... that was just their loss.

"By the way," Genevieve said, "Where have you guys been all this time? We were expecting help to be here days ago."

The Captain shook his head. "The world is a mess, Miss. We're doing all we can do. The cities were a priority. We were instructed to concentrate our efforts there."

"Lousy orders," Genevieve mumbled.

"Makes sense, I guess," Barney said with a shrug. "The rural areas should be able to take care of themselves better than those in the city. We have been doing some scavenging," Barney continued. "Are we going to get into trouble about that?"

"No. Not as long as you're taking truly abandoned goods for survival. Since we are in the area, do you need anything?"

When Genevieve opened her mouth to answer, the Captain smiled and raised his right hand. "Anything we might actually be able to help with."

"Oh. Can you get a doctor or someone to check on our ill? There is a lot of radiation sickness. We're losing people right and left."

The Captain called the medic over and sent him with Genevieve into the building. Genevieve came out a few minutes later, a grim look on her face. "It's as bad as I feared. We're going to lose most of those that are bad off already. Be more as time passes. According to the medic. He said there wasn't much to do except treat the symptoms and make them as comfortable as possible."

"I'm sorry," the Captain said. "It's the same all over. Too many people didn't understand the dangers and came out of shelter too soon, or just didn't have shelter to start with. Good shelter, anyway."

"Is there any chance we can get some diesel for the city water pump generator? At least we would have running water. It would be easier than trying to get fuel at the depot outside of town."

"Fuel is in short supply, just like everything else. You'd better take what you can get. We did fly over a tanker about ten miles out," the Captain said. "You might check it out and see if you can get it started. Assuming it isn't empty."

Genevieve turned her eyes to Barney. He was nodding. "So that's where the food is coming from!" she thought to herself. "Abandoned grocery delivery truck or trucks."

The helicopter was taking off and they fell silent due to the noise. "It will be back for us," the Captain said when it quieted down. "It's taking the bodies back to base. We'll take up residence until tomorrow in one of the abandoned buildings. We brought what we need, so don't worry about your own supplies. We'll leave anything we don't need behind for you to distribute."

The Captain turned then, and walked away without a further word. He joined the other

National Guardsmen and they went looking for a suitable building in which to spend the night. One of the men handed the Captain a back pack and he shrugged into it, taking the lead as the grouped moved off.

Genevieve looked over at Barney and asked, "What's our next project after we get that truck of food and the one of fuel back here?"

Barney wasn't surprised she'd figured it out, after the Captain mentioning the tanker. "Big... Giant garden plots. There were plenty of seed packets left in the hardware store, I noticed. We need to contact some of the ranchers and farmers around here, too. See where we can help them and they can help us. I'm surprised some of them haven't already been in. Surely an old tractor or something would have started after the attack, even with that EMP stuff you were talking about.

"And the bodies. We need to move the bodies from the shallow graves you've dug to the cemetery. They're a health hazard. I'm surprised the coyotes haven't started digging them up. I bet plenty of coyotes survived in their dens. I don't know. Look for more supply trucks before someone else gets to them. There're hundreds of things to get done."

"We'll manage," Genevieve said. She put her free arm through Barney's, much to his surprise. "We'll manage."

"You think we could maybe look for a beer truck, too?" Barney asked as they walked to-ward the City Hall building.

DON'T BUG ME
By
JERRY D. YOUNG

DON'T BUG ME

–

Prologue

Ronnie Cobb was a take advantage of everyone and everything, no-good, low-life, but he didn't deserve to die the way he did. Ronnie was the first in a long line of victims of what become known as the "Big Bug Invasion" by those involved.

But it wasn't really an invasion, at all. It was, in fact, a bio-genetic program gone horribly wrong. Due to negligence, in part, a lack of foresight, misunderstandings, and sheer bad luck, did the event start.

How do I know this? I was there, for the entire thing. And let me tell you, things could have been much worse. Only through the dedicated efforts of a handful of men was a worldwide disaster prevented and kept limited to a relatively small area.

Though I filed the story, just as it happened, with some names changed, it never saw print. I was told in no uncertain terms that what I had experienced had not actually happened. If I ever said otherwise, the powers that be would bring forth a whole string of experts to testify of my mental illness and the deranged ramblings to which I am prone.

So, the story here didn't really happen. There is no need to change any names, to protect the innocent, since the people in the story don't exist. Nor do the places described, or the Big Bugs.

John Needles, ex-reporter, new prepper, ranch hand in training.

CHAPTER ONE

-

"Hello John," said Dr. Marcel Kinsington. The two men shook hands. "I'm glad you were able to come out. I'm sorry it has taken so long to agree to the interview and discussion of our work here. It has just completed a key phase and I have a bit more time to devote to you than I would have earlier.

"That's fine, Dr. Kinsington. Work must come first," John replied, wanting to get on the man's good side.

"I go by Mark," said Kinsington.

"Mark, it is. What can you tell me about the project you are working on here?" John asked as they walked down a pristine hallway to Mark's office.

"We're quite proud of the work we are doing here. We are in the forefront of the development of genetically engineered beneficial insects for commercial farming operations."

1

"Isn't that a bit dangerous?" John asked. "What if something goes wrong?"

"Oh, we're quite security conscious around here. Both to protect our work from industrial espionage and to protect the environment from any possible contamination until we are ready to patent our creations and present them to farmers' worldwide."

When they reached Mark's office, both took seats. Mark behind the desk and John in front of it. John took a moment to peruse the many framed certificates lining the wall.

"Impressive collection," John told Mark, nodding at the wall.

"I have had the honor of attending, and later, teaching, at some of the finest institutes of learning in the world."

It struck John that there was a note of superiority in Mark's words and the way he stated them.

"So, you make beneficial bugs more beneficial…" John said to get Mark talking about his work. John had his digital tape recorder out, as well as his pad and pencil.

"No audio or video, I'm afraid," Mark said. "Security."

John nodded and turned off the recorder and put it in the pocket of his suit jacket. "No problem. Notes are okay, I hope. I don't have a Memorex memory."

Mark chuckled. "Oh, I don't think handwritten notes will compromise security. If I see you writing down proprietary information, I'll have you stop."

"Fair enough," John said. "The bugs?"

"Oh, yes. The bugs, as you put it. I suppose I should keep it simple. No long Latin names no one would recognize, anyway."

John smiled slightly. Mark, John decided, was very full of himself. "That would probably be best. I'm writing the article for the general public."

"Yes. No big words. Now, what particularly do you want to know?"

"I think first, how safe are these experiments?"

Mark frowned. "Quite safe, I assure you. If this is going to be a hatchet job, we can stop right here."

"No. No hatchet job. Just the truth. Surely there are concerns about safety?"

"Of course. We take safety here very seriously. Air locked vacuum rooms where the work is done to keep anything that might escape the work station vacuum chambers.

"The technicians wear sealed protective suits and are decontaminated each time they exit the work rooms. In a worst case scenario, the chambers can be flamed with a hydrogen and oxygen mix to incinerate any living thing inside. The whole room can get the same treatment, if it came to that. There is almost no danger of anything getting to the outside we don't want to get outside."

They were interrupted by a knock on the door, and its opening. "You want me to clean now, Boss?"

"Not now, Ronnie! What's the matter with you? I'm in the middle of an important interview."

"Sorry about that, Boss. Guess I'll go take my break and come back later."

"Please do so." Mark's voice was sharp. He turned to look at John again. "You know the saying about getting good help…"

John smiled and nodded. But that little interplay worried him. If the man wasn't good help why was he working in a potentially hazardous facility? John found out.

"Lay about, but he's my sister's husband. Keeping the work in the family." Mark grinned conspiratorially.

"Do tell. Back to the safety aspects of your operation…"

Mark cut him off. "I thought I covered that."

"Well, there are a couple more questions I have."

Reluctantly, it seemed to John, Mark said, "Very well. Please proceed."

"When you are ready to introduce the product, these beneficial bugs, what are the safeguards to make sure they don't just start eating the crops they are supposed to protect?"

Mark smiled. "I see I'm going to have to get very basic with you."

John didn't like the smirk that came with the statement, but held his tongue.

"We use bugs that don't eat crops. We're not changing their basic genetic makeup, only enhancing it. One of our engineered bugs that wouldn't eat the crops before we change it won't eat the crops after we change it."

"I see. That is reassuring. When do you think you'll have something to test?"

It was a huge grin on Mark's face when he spoke. "Oh, we're already in the testing stage. We had some early success and then accelerated the process. Come along. I'll show you what I mean."

John followed Mark silently to another part of the building. He used a card key to open a locked door with a biohazard sign on it. John hesitated. "Biohazard. Should we be suited up for this?"

"Nonsense," Mark said. "We're perfectly safe in here. Come along."

John followed Mark into the room and found rows of hydroponics tanks growing several different types of typical farm crops, from vegetables to cotton. "Take a close look. We've seeded the crops with invasive species of bugs." Mark stood aside and swung his arm in an inviting motion.

John leaned down and looked closely at a cotton plant. At first he didn't see anything. But then there was a motion from something tiny and he started to smile. Suddenly a bug the size of a silver dollar flew past his ear and pounced on the small bug crawling on the plant. It startled John and he jumped back.

Mark laughed. "What do you think of our little predatory bug?"

"I don't think it's little, for one thing," John said, edging back a bit closer to the cotton plant. The big bug flew off to another plant. "I don't remember anything from school about anything that big. At least, not here in the States."

"Oh, no. It's a cross of several different bugs, plus it's been genetically enhanced for size and appetite."

"What happens when they run out of invasive bugs to eat?" John asked.

"They die of starvation," Mark said.

"What if they decide to change their diet for other, say, beneficial insects."

Mark frowned. "The strains of bugs we merged were very specific as to their diet. Each one, in its natural genetic state only eats one thing."

"How did you get them to eat just what you want?"

Mark shook his head. "I believe it is probably over your head. We chose very specific attributes in the cross and then changed the DNA

6

to create a creature that only eats specific other bugs."

"I think I understand that," John said firmly. "It just seems like it would be difficult to limit something like that."

"It certainly was difficult," Mark replied, just as firmly. "This isn't some high school biology lab. It's taken me years of research and trial and error to achieve what I have."

John noted Mark's use of me and I. No mention of all the other scientists that were working with him. "I understand," John said and started to continue, but Mark cut him off.

"No, I don't think you do understand. I've done something remarkable here. In a few days the world will know just what it is. We have a field of soybeans behind the building that has had several invasive species of bug, as you call them, spread throughout. I was going to wait for some final results, but I'm sure enough of them that I will release the Predator V strain of attack bug."

"Wait. You mean out into the open? What about controls? What if it goes wrong?"

"Pshaw. I know these bugs like I know the back of my hand. Come along. You'll be the first to see."

Reluctantly, yet curious, John followed Mark out of the lab and into another. This one had shelf after shelf of cage after cage of the Predator V. John noticed immediately that they were bigger even that the bug he'd seen in the other lab. He said so.

"Yes. Of course they are. More aggressive, too. They'll even fight one another over a choice tidbit of food bug."

"Mark," John thought, "really likes that idea."

Mark opened a large tube and began to take the cages to the opening to dump the Predator V's into it. "Leads outside," Mark said in explanation. "Right to the soybean field."

"Are you sure you should be doing this without help at hand in case something goes wrong?"

"I must insist you stop raising unnecessary concerns about safety." Mark had emptied about half of the cages and closed the tube. "Now come along outside."

John had to admit, the swarm of Predator V's were doing their thing in the soybean field.

"Come back in three days and you'll see a completely bug free field. Good day."

Mark turned around and walked off. John knew a dismissal when he heard one. He headed for his Jeep, deciding this story could go on the back burner. "I guess," John said to himself, "I can go see if I can locate that survivalist group that's supposed to be around here."

John drove to town, to his motel and got on the computer. Fortunately, the motel offered free Wi-Fi so he was able to get on line without a problem. He opened up the file he'd started on the lab and put down the facts from his notebook, and then opened up the file on survivalists. It didn't have much in it.

Though he found a great deal of information, much of it marked and tagged to go back to at some time, John didn't find anything specific about a local survival MAG. "Time to pound the pavement," John said. "Just like the old days."

With a list of gun shops from the yellow pages, John headed out to do some journalistic sleuthing.

When he got back late the evening of the second day of searching out a MAG, he was tired, but happy with what he'd found. It was going to be a two birds with one stone kind of thing. The MAG was located not too far from the lab. "I bet they have a few choice things to say about the work going on there!" John thought before he went to bed.

The next morning John was up early, breakfasted, and on his way to the MAG compound he'd located the afternoon before. Having learned from earlier research that members of such groups were reporter shy, John had no intention of telling them he meant to do a story about them. Just that he wanted some help on the story about the lab.

When he pulled up to the gate of the property he stopped and tapped his horn twice, pause, twice more, pause, then three taps. The signal one of the gun shop owners told him would get someone to come down to see what he wanted.

A few minutes later a man showed up on a weird looking motorcycle. He stopped at the gate and asked John, who had stepped half out of the Jeep, what he wanted.

"I'm talking to people that live close to the lab up the road what they think about it and if they've had any trouble from it."

The man lifted a walky-talky to his lips and spoke. John couldn't hear what he said, but after listening to a response, the man pointed a remote control at a gate post and the gate rolled to one side.

"Follow me up to the main house," the man said and turned the back around to lead the way. It was only then that John saw the carbine slung across the man's back.

John looked around curiously as he followed the man on the motorcycle. He saw people here and there, going about many different tasks. Some were tending a large garden, others working with farm animals in a large field. He could hear the sounds of a chainsaw in the distance in a stand of trees to his left.

There were two men waiting for him on the porch of the large house the man on the motorcycle led him to. There were five other, slightly smaller houses on the property. John got out of the Jeep and walked up to the porch.

"You armed?" asked the man that had led him to the house.

John shook his head.

"That's okay Arley," said the taller of the two men on the porch. "I don't think he's going to be a problem."

John wasn't quite how to take the man's words. He went up the steps and shook hands with both men.

The big man introduced himself and the man standing beside him. "I'm Grant Neumont. This is by brother, Paver."

"John Needles," John replied. "I'm a reporter for…"

"I've read your stuff," Grant said. "That's why we let you in. You have questions about Marcel's lab?" He led the way inside the house and offered John a chair in the living room of the house.

"Yes," John replied. "You know him?"

"We've had words," Grant said. "When the lab was built. I'm not in favor of genetic manipulation of dangerous species. Not too much inclined to favor any genetic manipulation. What Marcel is doing is dangerous. He doesn't have sufficient safe guards to prevent one of his creatures from escaping, in my opinion. From what one our people saw, when she worked there for a while, the chance of something contaminating the experiments is high."

"I saw the facility. The air locks. Vacuum rooms and work booths. Isolation suits. Decontamination procedures."

"All very good," Grant replied. "Have they changed their procedures for entering the vacuum room?"

"I'm not sure. They suit up and go in. Is that the same?"

"That is. You noticed that yes, they decontaminate coming out, but not going in."

"Oh. Well… No, I guess they don't, John replied. "But the danger is something getting out, not in. Isn't it?"

"What happens if someone carries in something by accident and it contaminates what they're working on?"

"That would ruin an experiment. Wouldn't they just burn it and start over?"

"Would they? If they even knew? There are lots of things going on in that series of labs. Growth hormone research, for one. Other genetic research. Supposedly better food animals and crops. You put some of those things together and there is no telling what might happen."

"But if they keep everything isolated…"

"If," Grant replied. "If. When Ellie worked there for a while, that dufus that passes for a janitor went from one lab to the next, cleaning, never wearing an isolation suit. There is no telling what he carried from lab to lab."

"I saw him, I think," John said. "Mark's… Marcel's brother-in-law."

"That would explain it," Grant said. "From what Ellie has told me, he wouldn't be able to get a job anywhere if nepotism weren't involved."

Grant suddenly grinned. "Of course, I shouldn't talk about nepotism too much. I do a bit of it myself, here on the ranch."

"This is a ranch? Never would have known if you hadn't told me. I thought it was just a small residential development."

"Nice try, Reporter," Grant said with a small laugh. "We've been blindsided before about our beliefs. You won't get much, if anything, out of any of us."

John managed a small smile. He thought he had been pretty subtle. Grant was an astute character. Nothing like the human apes that most survivalists were supposed to be. "Well, I must say, you don't seem to fit the definition of survivalists."

"Not the MSM…" John looked questioningly at Grant. "That's Main Stream Media. Not the MSM definition, which has little or nothing to do with the core of the movement. The currently accepted definition only fits a small handful of extremists. In no way representative of the rest of us."

"So you are survivalists."

"Not by that definition," Grant said patiently. "We're preppers. We prepare for

13

disasters, natural or human-made. Prepping is just another form of insurance. For use when something bad happens."

"I see," John replied. "I'd like to learn more about it."

Paver spoke for the first time. "The Internet is full of Prep sites. Just Yahoo! the subject."

"Yahoo!? Not Google?" John grinned.

"Thin ice, there, Reporter," Paver said. "I happen not to like Google politics. I prefer Yahoo! Matter of personal choice. We aren't a bunch of redneck hicks here."

"I wasn't trying to give that impression," John replied. "I'm sorry if I did."

"Take it easy, Paver," Grant said with a chuckle. "I've read his stuff. He's okay. Not enough to pour out our hearts to, but okay."

"I appreciate that," John said. "And I must say, you've piqued my interest. I have done some research. On survivalists. I'll need to do more research on… what did you call it? Preps?"

"Preps. Prepping. Being prepared," Grant said. He gave John something of a sideways look. "I'm almost tempted to help you."

"Come on, Grant!" Paver said. "He's a reporter. Can't trust him any more than the last."

"Last?" John asked. "You've been interviewed before?"

"Not exactly," Grant said. "That ambush I was talking about. Leading questions, veiled accusations. Innuendo. She wanted a MSM, bible thumping, gun toting survivalist out to take down the government with terror tactics. She left without much information."

"Real witch, she was," Paver added.

A young woman put her head around the door jamb. "Pappa? You want coffee for our guest?"

"Sure, sweetie," Grant said without looking around. "Coffee, Mr. Needles? Tea? Fresh from the cow milk?"

"Coffee is fine," John said. "And please. Call me John."

"Very well, John," Grant said. "Now, understanding that you want a story, what assurances can you give me that this isn't just a hatchet job in the making?"

"If you've read my work, I think you can make that decision on your own."

"Grant…" Paver said, ready to object.

"Come on, Paver," Grant said, cutting his brother's words off. "Wouldn't it be nice to have a truthful accounting of some preppers?" He looked at John then. "No names or identifying information."

"Agreed," John quickly replied.

"What do you want to know?" Grant asked.

They paused for a moment as the young woman carried in a tray with a coffee and tea service. She poured three cups and then hurried out, Grant's words following her. "Thank you, Tiffany."

"Oh, man!" John said, "This is great coffee!"

Grant smiled. "We grow our own here, roast it and grind it fresh for each pot."

"You can grow coffee here?"

"Special greenhouse we keep for specialty plants like coffee," Paver said proudly.

"Don't get much production, but it gives all of us a taste now and again, for those that drink coffee."

"Oh," John said. "You probably shouldn't be wasting it on me."

"Company gets the best we have," Grant said.

"Well, thank you. I appreciate that," John said, and meant it.

"Go ahead and ask your questions," Grant said. "If you bring up something that is off limits we'll just say so. Don't try to pursue it and we'll be fine."

"How did you get involved in the movement?" John asked, pulling his pencil and pad from a pocket.

"We're not too involved with any movement," Grant said easily, after taking a sip of the coffee. "We are fairly active on some forums, giving our opinions for the most part, based on our experience, but what group we have is immediate and extended family."

John nodded. "But you had to start somewhere. What got you interested in surv… Preparedness?"

"Being a rancher, being prepared for natural disasters came pretty natural. As did putting up food by home canning. My father lived through the Cuban Missile Crisis. Made a small shelter in the basement of the original house here, according to plans in a Civil Defense booklet I brought home from school. That was the start of the family's prepping for human caused disasters."

"I see. So you've been doing this for a long time."

"Not as the project and lifestyle it has become, but in a very basic way, yes."

"As a lifestyle?"

"Yes. We live a prepared lifestyle here. We do many things, as a matter of course that were originally thought of as a specific part of preps. Now they are just part of our everyday activities."

"Such as?" John asked.

"Keeping up with the weather news, which we have always done, for the obvious reason of being a working ranch. But we also keep pretty close watch on local, state, regional, national, and international news. By broadcast TV, but also by listening to Shortwave stations almost every day."

"And Amateurs," Paver said.

"Amateurs?" John asked. "Amateurs at what?"

Grant smiled. "Amateur Radio Operators. Often called Hams."

"Oh. Hams. That I understand."

Paver added a bit more. "They are a good source of information you won't hear or see from MSM."

"What else do you do daily?" John asked.

"Always conscious of security," Grant said. "Shop for food, that we don't produce ourselves, with long term storage in mind."

"Security," John said slowly. "Do you have guns?"

"We do," Grant said easily. "Several of us carry a handgun all the time when we're out and about on the property."

"I see."

"I'm not sure you do," Paver said. "We work with large animals every day. Get caught out in a pasture around a bull, or between a cow and her calf, or a sow and her piglets… Things can get serious quickly."

"And we have coyotes trying to get to the young stock and the chickens," Grant added.

"So the guns are for protection from your animals and wild animals. Not people."

"Oh, they are for protection against bad people. We had an escapee from the prison take up residence in our firewood coppice area. He'd had a gun smuggled in and killed a guard getting away from the work gang. We found him and held him until the State Police could come take him off our hands." Grant gave a little shrug and added, "We carry for protection from four legged and two legged problems.

"Did you shoot him?" John asked.

"No, we didn't shoot him!" Paver said. "Grant got the drop on him and didn't have to shoot him. We use the minimum level of force we need to accomplish whatever goal we have. We don't use an elephant gun to kill a rabbit."

"Don't use guns at all, unless it's absolutely necessary," Grant said, giving Paver a cautioning look. "They are just another tool we use, just like a hammer or tractor."

"What crops do you grow?" John asked.

"A variety. Hay for one, for the stock and to sell a little. Wheat to sell and to get straw. Soybeans, another commercial crop, plus oil for our biodiesel operation. Corn, mostly for silage and feed corn for the farm. We sell a little. Turnips as a cover crop and food use for the family.

"Then there are the truck farm crops. Vegetables, melons, strawberries, blackberries and the fruits and nuts from our orchard. And our greenhouse products. Besides the coffee we grow some exotics for our own use. Miniature bananas and citrus, plus some more vegetables, and our primary winter crop, salad vegetables."

Grant and Paver both noticed that John was writing everything down as he listened. Catching up with what Grant had told him, John asked,

"What about animals? You said you had fresh milk."

"From a small dairy herd. We also ranch beef cattle, swine, chickens for eggs and meat, and fish in the greenhouse tanks. It all goes to a local dairy or meat processor."

"From the looks of things, you do okay."

"Thank you. Our family has been farming and ranching on this land for five generations. We've learned what works and what doesn't. We're proud of our 'green' efforts to help the environment and our almost off-grid existence."

"That is interesting," John said and meant it. But he had to say, "I wish I could stay longer, but I'm supposed to meet Mark to see how his latest experiment goes."

"What's he working on now?" Pave asked. "More magic bugs?"

John smiled. "So to speak. He's released a strain of anti-bug bugs into his soybean field that he'd seeded with invasive bugs."

John saw Grant's eyes widen slightly. "He's put some of his creations into the environment?"

John nodded.

"This could be bad," Grant said.

"This is bad!" said Paver.

"Well, I guess I'll find out soon enough." John got up and reached for Grant's hand.

Grant held his hand out and the two men shook. A bit reluctantly, Paver shook hands with John when John offered it. "Thank you for the coffee and your time. I'd like to come back later and get more information, if I might."

Grant was showing John the door. "On a condition," Grant said.

John didn't like conditions being put on him, but he asked, "And what would that be?"

"That you do a thorough decontamination of yourself and wear different clothes than what you wear to the lab."

"Oh," John replied, expecting something else entirely. "I can do that. You really are worried about what Mark is doing, aren't you?"

"I think it shows," Grant said.

"Good-bye and thank you for your time. It may be a couple of days before I get back here. I hope that is okay."

"Decontaminated in the meantime," Paver said firmly.

John nodded and got in his Jeep to leave. He saw Paver lift a handheld radio to his lips and assumed Paver was telling Arley to let John out. The thought passed through his mind that no one knew where he was, and if Arley was getting orders to detain him, there wasn't much John could do about it.

But the gate was open and Arley gave a friendly wave as John passed.

Fifteen minutes later John pulled into the parking lot of the lab. He walked into the office and asked for Mark. The receptionist looked a bit upset. "He's busy."

"He asked me to come back to see him, today."

"He's busy. He doesn't want to be disturbed."

"I see," John said and turned to leave. When he went outside, on a whim, he headed for the back of the lab where the soybean field was. "That's odd," he muttered upon seeing the Mark and another man, apparently his brother in law, going through the field with a butterfly net and one of the cages.

"Mark!" John called out and headed for the field.

Mark looked up and saw John. "Go away! Come back in a week!"

John slowed his pace but then Ronnie let out a scream and began running toward the edge of the soybean field. John ran to where Ronnie would exit the field. Mark was making his way there, too.

Ronnie slapped something and John thought a cat had jumped on his back. But it was no cat. Whatever it was flew away. Ronnie made it to the edge of the field and went down, slapping at more of whatever it was that was attacking him.

When John got a bit closer he realized that it was the Predator V's all over Ronnie. John came to a sliding stop. He just realized that the bugs were three times the size of the ones Mark had released.

Ronnie screamed again and writhed on the ground, trying to crush the bugs under him or sweep them away with his hands. But it wasn't working. Mark got to Ronnie the same time John got there.

"Get the cage! Get the cage!" Mark yelled and snagged one of the bugs with the butterfly net.

John went into the field far enough to recover the cage that Ronnie had dropped. If there'd been anything in it, it was long gone. The cage had landed on its side and the door flipped open.

John held the cage and let Mark empty the butterfly net into it. There was no longer any sound coming from Ronnie. Mark kept transferring the Predator V bugs from Ronnie to the cage. There were only three left when one of them left Ronnie and landed on John.

It was all he could do not to scream in pain and drop the cage as the bug's sharp mandibles tore a hole through John's pants' leg and into his flesh. "Get it off! Get it off!"

Mark turned to him and grabbed the bug with his bare hand and threw it into the cage. Two more grabs and all the visible bugs were captured, leaving Ronnie a bloody mess on the ground.

"What happened?" John asked, carefully putting down the cage, and going to one knee to check on Ronnie. "Are those the same bugs you released three days ago?" John felt for a pulse in Ronnie's neck. Nothing.

After rolling Ronnie over, John lifted one of his eyelids. Just a blank stare. Ronnie was dead. John said as much.

"He can't be!" Mark said loudly. "The Predator V's aren't capable of attacking anything except small invasive bugs!"

"Well, they sure were attacking Ronnie," John said, turning his attention to the bite on his leg. "I want to get this washed out and something on it. It's beginning to burn."

"That's the Predator's venom."

"Venom? They're poisonous?"

"Only to other insects… Normally," Mark replied. "But… come inside. We have a first-aid kit."

"You haven't answered me, Dr. Kinsington," John said as he limped behind Mark, the casual mood gone completely. "Are those… things… the ones you released three days ago?"

"Yes. Yes. They are. If you must know. And I must remind you that you can't say anything about this."

"But a man is dead! We have to notify the authorities."

"No! I'll handle this." Mark led the way into a back door in the lab and to a small lab room. There was a first-aid kit on the wall and Mark removed it.

John sat down in the only chair in the room and Mark tended to the bite, cutting a large flap in John's slacks to get to the skin.

"Geez!" John groaned. "That hurts worse than the bite.

"I have to get as much of the venom out as I can. It shouldn't be affecting you at all. Something has changed the Predator V's."

"You think?" John asked sarcastically as Mark positioned a large pad bandage on the site of the bite.

"I'm going to call the police," John said, standing up and stepping to the telephone on the wall.

"No!" Mark said. "You aren't."

John looked around and saw the small semi-automatic pistol Mark was pointing at him.

"Aw! Come on! You have to be kidding!" John lifted his arms even with his shoulders when Mark made a motion with the gun.

"Over there." Mark made a motion toward a door to one side of the room.

John opened the door. It was a closet. "Now, wait a minute!"

Mark gave John a shove, closed the door, and locked it all before John could react.

"Hey! Open this door!" John yelled, throwing his weight against the door. It was fruitless. John kicked the door in exasperation.

"Criminey!" he said a few seconds later. He took out his cell phone and tried to call out. No signal. The steel reinforced construction of the lab was blocking the signal. He kicked the door again.

John finally sat down on the floor and made himself as comfortable as possible. And waited. He checked his watch every few minutes, fuming as the time passed. After an hour and a half in the closet, he heard someone in the lab outside the door.

"Hey! Let me out of here!" John called, banging on the door with a fist.

The door suddenly opened and John blinked at the bright lights of the lab, his eyes adjusted to the near total darkness of the closet. It was the receptionist. She looked terrified to John.

"Where's Dr. Kinsington?" John asked.

"Outside! Something is wrong. The phones don't work and everyone is outside. They told me to stay inside. I'm scared."

John went to the wall phone. No dial tone. John didn't think it was a coincidence. He pulled out his cell phone again.

"Cell phones don't work in this building," the receptionist said.

"I'll go outside and use it," John said. "What is your name?"

"Priscilla Harding."

"Okay, Priscilla. Don't worry. I'll figure out what is going on." John hurried toward the front of the lab building and went outside. He got three bars of signal strength. With a sigh of relief, he dialed 911.

When the dispatcher answered, John said, "There is an emergency at the research lab out on…"

"Sir," the female dispatcher said, "There is a significant penalty for fake 911 calls. I suggest you hang up and think about what you are trying to do." She hung up.

"She hung up on me!" John said, turning a stunned look on Priscilla, who was standing in the entrance of the lab building, holding the door half open.

John shook his head and then ran around to the back of the lab. There were the other lab workers. They, with Dr. Kinsington, were in the process of capturing more of the Predator V's. John slowed to a stop. It seemed that they were having success.

And to his surprise, there was Ronnie, working alongside the other. "You were dead!" John exclaimed when he came up to the group. Ronnie didn't answer. Dr. Kinsington did.

"You've been out of your head. Ronnie is fine. The bugs are fine."

"I was attacked by one of those things!" John insisted. "Look at my leg."

"You had that when you got here," Dr. Kinsington insisted. There is no problem here."

"Yeah, and these aren't the droids you're looking for. Move along. Something is going on here!"

"Droids? What on earth are you talking about?" Dr. Kinsington said. "You should go home and take a rest."

"You've obviously never seen Star Wars. And one thing I can see for myself right now is those bugs are three times the size they were when you released them."

"You are quite mistaken," replied Dr. Kinsington, netting another of the bugs.

John didn't know what to do. He was sure he wasn't crazy, but there was Ronnie, perfectly fine.

Dr. Kinsington gave John a hard look. "I must ask you to leave. We have important work to do."

"I'll be back," John replied and turned on his heal to leave. "That's another movie quote, by the way."

John went back to the motel and plopped down on the bed. "I know I'm not imagining this." Bouncing off the bed he left the motel room and headed for the police station.

"I need to report some suspicious goings on at the lab out on…"

"Get lost, buddy. We've been warned about you. I'm doing you a favor. If I let you make the report I'll just have to arrest you for making a false police report, and for harassing Dr. Kinsington."

"Kinsington called and warned you about me?" John asked, shocked.

"That he did. Said you were trying to get the lab shut down and were telling tall tales about monster bugs and dead bodies. I suggest you go take one of your Valiums or whatever your psychiatrist has you on for your delusions."

"I am not delusional!" John said, louder than he intended. The look on the desk sergeant's face was enough warning for John to turn and leave before he got arrested. He went back to the motel.

"I know what I saw!" John said aloud. "Something is going on there. I'm sure of it." He pulled his computer out of its case and went on-line. "There has to be something I missed," he muttered as he looked for additional information on Dr. Marcel Kinsington.

Finding nothing useful, John went out to get some supper. When he got back to the motel he had determined to continue to look into the situation. Give it a couple of days, and then go back to the lab. Perhaps in the dark.

John gave it a few days and then went back to the lab, under cover of darkness. There didn't seem to be anyone around, but he was no B&E specialist. He didn't even try to get in. He did look around the outside of the building for unlocked doors, but found none. He went out to the soybean field and looked around with a flashlight. John checked several of the plants closely in the light from the flashlight. No signs of invasive bugs, or of the Predator V's, big or little.

"Maybe I was dreaming it… No! I know what I saw!" John muttered to himself and then went back to his Jeep, to return to the motel. He was going to have to decide what to do soon. He was running out of expense money for the two stories.

"Best go back and see the preppers tomorrow and call it good," John said to himself and went to bed after a light supper.

John was parked at the gate of the Neumont property and gave the horn signal again. A few moments later Arley opened the gate and waved John through, then disappeared into the trees on his funny looking motorcycle.

It was almost a duplicate of the scene of a few days earlier. Grant and Paver were waiting on the porch of the house and welcomed him back to the ranch. Grant didn't lead them into the house. Instead, he and Paver stepped down off the porch. Grant asked, "What did you find out at the lab?"

"That's… kind of confusing…" John said slowly. Not quite understanding why he was telling Grant and Paver what had happened, he did so. About Ronnie's death… Supposedly. And the attack on John. He showed them the marks after he took the bandage off.

"Could have been anything done that," Paver said.

"Yeah," John said. "But it wasn't 'anything.' It was one of the Predator V's. Things were big as cats."

"Cats?" Grant asked.

"Look!" John insisted, at the look Grant gave him. "I am not making this up!"

They'd been walking down to one of the several barns on the property and continued to talk as Grant checked on a few things.

"I'm inclined to believe you. But Kinsington has a lot of pull around here. Didn't bring a lot of jobs with him for the lab, but the people he brought in do spend their money in town."

"I don't know what to do," John admitted. "They've already discredited me. Unless I can get some hard evidence…"

"Well," Grant said slowly, "We might just be able to help you with that. Do you think they got all the bugs when they were rounding them up?"

John shook his head. "I don't see how they could have. That's a big field. I just don't think they could have found every one of them, even as big as they are."

"What say we pay a little visit to the property? Check on that soybean field ourselves," Grant said. "I've got a lot to protect here, and I aim to do it, if that loon has turned something dangerous into the environment."

"You'd go with me?" John asked, surprised.

"Sure. Why not?" Paver asked. "We are as concerned about the environment as anyone. Maybe more so than most."

"Aw, Cool down, Paver," Grant said. "You need to mellow out. John is okay."

"Yeah. Well… I'm going up to the house to get something besides my pistol."

"Guns?" John asked.

Paver gave him a pitying look, and Grant smiled slightly. "You want one?" he asked.

John started to say, vehemently, no, but he thought about the size of the bugs and the pain of that first bite. And the fact that Kinsington had pulled a gun on him. "Yeah. I think I will. What do you have?"

"Oh, we have a selection," Grant replied, still smiling. "Paver, get him a Glock 21 and half a dozen magazines."

"Grant, are you sure…"

Grant gave his brother a look and Paver headed back to the house. Grant, satisfied with the operation in the barn, led John back to the house more slowly.

Paver handed Grant two long guns and turned to John. The decision made, Paver carefully led John through the workings of the Glock. "It's simple. Rack the slide to chamber a round, squeeze the trigger. There are no external safeties. Just aim and squeeze.

"When the magazine is empty, the slide will lock back. Push this button to drop the spent magazine and slide a full one in, firmly. Press down on this small button and the slide will go forward, chambering another round and it'll be ready for another trigger pull.

"Do not, under any circumstances, put your finger on the trigger until you are ready to shoot. That little lever you see in the trigger is the safety. If it is flush with the trigger, the trigger will pull.

"Here's a belt, holster, and magazine carriers with six loaded magazines. Ninety-one rounds total."

"I doubt we'll need these," John said. "Though Kinsington did pull a pistol on me."

"So you said. Come on. Let's go." Grant led the way to a light gray Suburban SUV parked in the house parking lot. Paver got into the front passenger seat and John took the back seat and buckled up.

It was only a fifteen-minute drive to get to the lab. There were several cars in the lot, and Grant parked in the slot nearest the front door. "Let's take a look out back, first," Grant said, leaving the Suburban.

The three walked around the building to take a look at the soybean field. There were three people there, two with fish nets, and one with one of the cages.

"They were using butterfly nets before," John said.

Suddenly the back door of the lab opened and a man stuck his head out to yell, "Get in here! We need help! Another batch transformed!"

Before anyone could do anything, the man screamed and fell in the door. The door was held open by the man's body as he writhed in pain. It was a bit difficult to see, but there was movement on the man's back.

As the lab techs ran up, so did Grant, Paver, and John.

"I thought you said they were the size of cats!" Grant exclaimed, taking careful aim with a pistol that was suddenly in his hands. He fired and the bug went tumbling without a sound. "That thing is as big as a big dog!"

"No!" yelled one of the techs. "You can't kill them. We have to capture them."

"Tell that to the dead guy," Paver said, as he stood back up. "Thing ripped him open in the back. The skin is burned like acid burns."

The three lab techs looked back and forth at each other and to their dead colleague. Without a word, all three turned and ran toward the front of the building, dropping the nets and cage.

"Hey!" John yelled, but dived back out of the way as a dozen of the big bugs flew through the partially open door. They didn't fly far, but seemed to land, hop, and then fly again.

"Close it! Close it! Close it!" Grant yelled. He dropped to the ground and pulled the dead lab tech out of the way and Paver closed the door, leaning against it to hold it closed until the lock latched.

When the screams came, Grant, Paver, and John all ran toward the front of the building. The three lab techs were under attack by the bugs. "Get the shotguns!" Grant yelled to Paver and then advanced on the closest man. He was trying to fight off two of the bugs.

Careful not to hit the tech, Grant aimed and fired three times. Both bugs fell away from the man. John got a look at his face as the man collapsed. His face was ripped viciously, as was his belly. There was blood spurting in several places.

"Come on!" Grant said. "Snap out of it. He's dead." He advanced on the other man and fired.

John heard a shotgun boom and one of the bugs now bounding and flying toward Paver disappeared in a spray of bug parts. John looked around and one of the bugs had left a lab tech and was coming for him.

Feeling infinitely slow and awkward, John pulled the Glock from the holster on the borrowed belt and fired at the bug just as it landed, in preparation of bouncing up to fly again. John was well aware that it had been a lucky shot, but it gave him confidence and he advanced side by side with Grant, firing at the other bugs. Paver was doing his part with the shotgun.

The bugs seemed to understand where the danger to them was coming from and all the remainder left the bodies of the lab techs and launched an attack on the three men firing at them.

The last one flew into John, but it was dead, with one of Grant's bullets in it.

Following Grant's and Paver's examples, John reloaded the Glock before he did anything other than look around for any additional bugs.

"Okay," Grant said. "This is going to be bad. But there could be people alive in there. And we need to destroy every one of the bugs we can find before more of them get out."

Paver nodded. It was a second or so, but John nodded, too. Grant holstered his pistol and took the second shotgun, which Paver had slung over his back while using the other one.

"Let's see if we can get in," John said, taking the first steps to the front door of the lab building. He almost got sick when he looked through the glass and saw two of the bugs devouring the body of Priscilla.

"Don't let it get to you, man," Grant said. "This is the Doctor's responsibility, not ours."

Paver looked a little green around the gills, too, but stepped forward when Grant grasped the handle of the door. When he opened it, Paver and John stepped inside and began firing. It was over before Grant could get inside.

But a bug came running from one of the hallways, and all three men fired at once. It disintegrated from the two shotgun rounds and single forty-five slug from John's Glock. Ears ringing from the shots in the enclosed space, they didn't hear the screams coming from deeper in the lab for a moment. When they did hear them, the three ran down the hallway, guns up and ready.

When they got close they realized that there was more than one person screaming. Paver, a step ahead, opened and went through the door from behind which the closest screams were coming. The shotgun boomed, but Grant and John were advancing down the hallway.

Grant nodded at the next door, though there was no sound coming from it. Grant continued toward the other screams. John opened the door and almost lost his head. The bug was clinging to the wall above the door and made a swipe at John with one foreleg covered in razor sharp spikes.

But the bug wasn't silent when it moved and John heard the motion and dived to the floor, sustaining a painful scratch across his shoulders, but still with his head attached. Scooting backwards on his rear, John lifted the Glock and fired three times as the bug leaped toward him. John was covered in green bug slime when he rolled out from under the dead bug.

Climbing to his feet, John checked behind the counter in the lab. Another dead lab tech, this one almost completely consumed. He heard more firing and carefully left the lab he was in, so as not to get shot by accident.

He moved down the hallway and suddenly squatted down when Grant yelled, "Incoming! One got past me!"

It wasn't trying to fly, John saw. It was running a funny, six-legged gait. But it was fast. It was almost on him when John hit it with his third shot. John quickly reloaded. The shot that had killed the bug just before it got to him had been the last one in the magazine.

"It's me!" Grant called out and stepped around the corner of the hallway.

"Me, too!" said Paver, joining them from one of the labs between them.

"What do you think?" Paver asked. "We get them all?"

"I don't know," Grant replied. "We just reacted to the screams. You find anyone alive?"

Paver and John both shook their heads.

"Okay. Let's check the rest of the place…" Grant was speaking when a flurry of scrabbling sounds came around the far corner of the lab, from the reception area.

All three men spun, but more sound came from behind them.

"They've trapped us!" Paver said, turning toward the bugs further in the lab. John and Grant began firing at the five bugs approaching from the reception area. Paver did the same behind them.

The hallway was littered with slippery, slimy, smelly bug guts when the firing stopped.

Grant and Paver were covered in the slime now, too, just as John was.

"How you doing for ammunition?" Grant asked, as the three stood back to back.

"Still have ten rounds for the shotgun and thirty-nine for my Glock," Paver replied.

"Three clips left," John said.

"Magazines," said both Paver and Grant.

"Three magazines," John said.

"I'm down to five shotgun shells and a single magazine for my Glock. I think we'd better make a strategic retreat, get some more ammunition, and decide what we do next."

Grant carefully led the way toward the reception area again, trying not to slip in all the slime. It was difficult. But they made it without falling or running into any additional bugs. "You don't think these things can open doors, do you?" John asked as they went out the front door.

"They can this one," Paver said. "It's a push to open. But surely they can't open the doors with regular door knobs. Can they?"

"I don't know," John said. "One laid for me above the door of one of the rooms. And I think that last attack was orchestrated."

"Intelligence?" Grant asked.

"More likely instinct. I don't know enough about bugs to even guess what insects they started with. If any were social and worked together as a matter of course."

"Guess it doesn't matter," Grant said after a pause. "We must assume some intelligence. They've sure shown it, or a good facsimile of it. Let's find something to block these doors. Paver, get the rope out of the Suburban. And some more ammunition."

"What if there are more people in there?" John asked.

Before Grant could answer, three more bugs charged the door. But they weren't after the door, not initially. They were chasing Dr. Kinsington. Kinsington was firing back over his shoulder with his small automatic.

John grabbed the door and flung it open as Grant raised the shotgun. "Down! Down, Doc!"

Either he was too panicked or simply didn't hear Grant, but Kinsington continued to run. Grant only had a shot at one of the bugs and took it. The other two were behind Kinsington and Grant couldn't get a good shot at either of them.

Both bugs leaped and landed on Dr. Kinsington, one slashing down his back with mandibles and forelegs, and the other on the doctor's head. Grant couldn't shoot either one of them with the shotgun without hitting the doctor. He started drawing his Glock.

John lifted his pistol and fired at the one on the doctor's head, killing it and knocking it off the doctor. But it was already too late when Grant shot the other bug in the process of ripping the doctor's back. Dr. Kinsington was dead.

Paver came running up and handed Grant and John three filled magazines each, and Grant a box of shotgun shells. Grant holstered the pistol and put the magazines in the empty pouches on his belt. He reloaded the shotgun as John added the magazines Paver had given him to his own empty magazine pouches.

"Okay. We can't wait, I guess," Grant said. "There could be more in here. Let's lock the doors and go through the place, locking doors behind us, until we've cleared the entire building."

John and Paver both nodded. Grant closed and locked the front doors from inside. "John stay here and cover the doors in here. Paver and I will go the same way we did before. Kill what we find or drive them into here. You okay with that?"

John nodded.

"Good man," Grant said. "Let's go, Paver. Forget the rope. We'll lock from inside until we get back here."

It was like being on pins and needles, John decided, standing there, gun held down in front of him in a two-hand hold, just waiting. He jumped once when one of the shotguns fired. And then again when three quick shots were fired from one of the pistols.

He hesitated for a fraction of a second when a bug came out of the far hallway, but he got the gun up and fired twice before the bug spotted him and started forward. Three more times lone bugs came into the reception area and John put them down.

"Don't fire, John!" Grant called out, his voice coming from the hallway from which the bugs had come.

"Come on out. Everything is okay in here," John responded.

"I'm going to get the first aid kit out of the Suburban," Paver said. "This scratch is burning."

"Okay, Paver. We're right behind you. Come on, John. I think we got them all." Grant unlocked the front doors to let Paver out and ushered John out, too.

As Paver went over to the Suburban, John helped Grant tie the doors firmly closed, just in case. The task done, the two went over and began to treat each other's sundry cuts, scrapes, and bites.

"You hear that?" Grant suddenly asked, cocking his head slightly and putting one hand up behind his ear to amplify the sound.

"Quick decision. That's choppers on the way in. Dollars to donuts someone did call someone of importance about this. We stay or go? Paver?"

"Let's boogie."

"John?"

"I should stay. There's a story here that…"

"Okay. Paver and I are out of here. Keep our names out of it."

"Wait," John said, looking toward the now obvious sound of approaching helicopters. "I'm going with you, if that is okay."

"Get in," Grant said. The three scrambled into the Suburban and Grant took off. Paver and John were watching for the helicopters. They were on the road, well on the way toward the Neumont compound when the sound of the helicopters changed. They were landing.

"I don't think they made us," Paver said.

"I don't know," Grant said. "If they were looking, they saw us. We'll just have to wait it out and see what happens."

Grant turned slightly in his seat and looked at John in the rear seat. "You feel like a short vacation. A few days at the ranch. Might be a story in it."

John smiled. "I can handle that."

"You know," Paver said a few minutes later. "I think I solved your dead Ronnie puzzle. I found a body just like you described. Been in cold storage, but it was obvious it had been dead a few days. But there was another body, fresh, that matched it. I think Ronnie had a twin brother."

"That would explain it," John said. He'd been trying to figure out that point ever since Ronnie had apparently come back to life.

JERRY D. YOUNG

DON'T BUG ME
-
Epilogue

It was a week before anyone left the ranch. No one had come by asking questions. When John drove past the lab… or, actually, the bare ground where the lab and soybean field had been, he decided he'd made the right decision. To get involved. He was thinking that Grant and Paver and their family had some pretty good ideas. Big bugs hadn't been on their list of things to prepare for, Grant had told him, before all this happened. It was now.

Another week went by before John submitted the story, or a version of it, to his paper. No mention was made of Grant or Paver or the ranch. "Unknown persons, passing through," was the term John used to refer to the help he had dealing with the situation. An hour after he transferred the story to his editor, two guys in black suits and mirrored sunglasses showed up at the paper and asked to talk to John.

John went quietly, listened to the harangues and threats, not answering any questions along the way. A day later he was released, not having been charged with anything. He went back to the paper. His desk was already occupied by someone, and his final check was waiting for him. John decided to change careers.

THANK YOU FOR READING

"SURVIVAL SHORT STORIES: BOOK 2"

By

Jerry D. Young

LIKE THIS BOOK?

See more great books at www.creativetexts.com

"OZARK RETREAT"

"BUGGING HOME"

"THE SLOW ROAD"

"LOW PROFILE"

"RUDY'S PREPAREDNESS SHOP"

"CME: CORONAL MASS EJECTION"

"HOME SWEET BUNKER"

"THE HERMIT"

& MANY MORE GREAT PAW FICTION & OTHER
TITLES

THANK YOU!

MEET THE AUTHOR

Jerry D Young was born at home, in Senath, Missouri July 3, 1953. At age 5 the family rented a small farm house on an active farm 40 miles southwest of St. Louis. While the family weren't farmers, they lived something of a homestead type life, raising a milk cow, sometimes two, and calves, a pig or two, chickens, and the occasional goat. Along with the stock, a large garden helped to feed Jerry's three brothers and two sisters for several years. Fishing and hunting contributed to the pantry, as did foraging the wild edibles on the property.

At the age of 14, the family, minus a brother and two sisters that were now adults and on their own, moved back to Senath. Having been encouraged from an early age to read, Jerry was a regular patron of the Senath Branch Library.

A love of a good story was born within him, and shortly before graduating high school, for a lack of stories that he liked at the library, he began to write short vignettes, and started taking notes for stories that he wanted to tell. Jerry eventually began to write in earnest and now has more than 100 titles to his credit including Prep/PAW stories, Action/Adventure, and a few of the romance type stories that first got him started.